End Play

-A Sarah Stone Thriller-

by

Iain Rob Wright

END PLAY

A Sarah Stone Thriller

Copyright © 2017 by Iain Rob Wright

All rights reserved. No part of this book may be reproduced in any form by any electronic or mechanical means including photocopying, recording, or information storage and retrieval without permission in writing from the author.

ISBN-13: 978-1520521664

Cover art by Stuart Bache
Images by Shutterstock
Edited by Autumn Speckhardt
Interior design by Iain Rob Wright

www.iainrobwright.com

Give feedback on the book at:
iain.rorbert.wright@hotmail.co.uk

Twitter: @iainrobwright

First Edition

Printed in the U.S.A

To my fans,
you guys rule!

"The war against terrorism is terrorism."

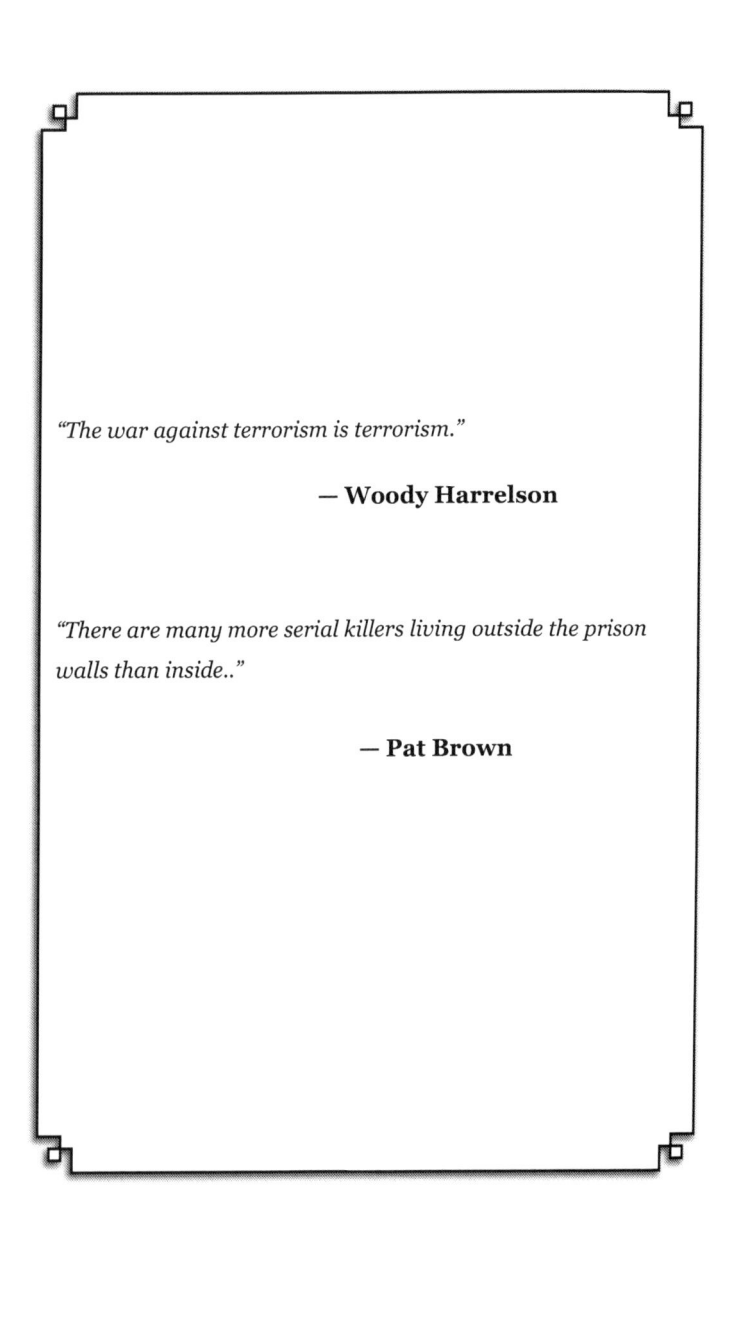

— **Woody Harrelson**

"There are many more serial killers living outside the prison walls than inside.."

— **Pat Brown**

Chapter 1

Sarah dodged the London traffic and descended the muddy embankment beside the road. Even in heavy boots she risked slipping, but Howard's hand against her back kept her steady.

"Remind me what this tip-off said?" she asked, wincing as she nearly twisted her ankle.

"It wasn't really a tip-off," Howard told her. They reached the bottom of the hill, and he let go of her shoulder. "Local bus driver broke down and saw someone skulking around this ditch. When he asked if they needed help, the stranger fled."

Sarah rolled her eyes. She imagined the drivers passing by thinking what an idiot she was tramping about in the mud. "Palu only has us following this because we have zero other leads."

"And two of the victims were found in inner-city ditches like this," said Howard.

Sarah glanced back at the main road. Like most of London in the morning, it was chock-a-block, and exhaust fumes billowed in the air. "I hate this city," she muttered.

Howard stepped up beside her.

"Nothing. Come on, let's check it out fast. It stinks down here."

Howard tugged up his belt, raising his trouser cuffs away from the mud. "You okay? You look pissed off—even more than normal."

"I'm fine. I just don't..." Sarah's words faded. Something about the way Howard looked at her—like he actually cared—made her want to open up to him. She almost spilled herself open: No, I'm not fine, Howard. Ever since I met you, I've been battered and bruised, almost killed a dozen times, and forced to watch my friends die. I don't sleep. Every loud noise makes me curl up beneath the covers. Oh yeah, and my dead husband just returned and wants to act like nothing happened—like I didn't lose half of my face and a baby back in that desert. I am not fine, Howard. So, help me, please. Instead, she shrugged. "Better things to do then trudge through mud, Howard. Let's just get this over with."

He shrugged. "All right. You want to take point?"

"Yeah." She examined the way ahead. The ditch cut alongside the road to collect runoff from a row of cement culverts. The ground was a quagmire, thick with scum of iridescent foam where chemical pollution from nearby factories mixed with rain and sewer water. An animal corpse rotted a few metres away, a scrawny grey thing that could have been a fat squirrel or a skinny badger. Sarah pictured a stranger skulking around down here and decided it was unusual enough to investigate—but by some local plod, not a pair of MCU agents. What was Palu doing sending them here?

Thinking of her ex-husband—or husband again now, she considered—forced a rush of anxiety into the pit of Sarah's stomach. The sensation was less akin to butterflies, and closer to a swarm of locusts.

"You think these pipes lead into the sewer?" asked Howard, pointing to the line of culverts.

"I don't know," she admitted—plumbing wasn't one of her skills. "I remember playing in pipes like that when I was a kid though, pretending to be an SAS soldier to impress my dad."

She nearly laughed at the memory, but it died before it passed her lips. Howard knew better than to prod for details about her childhood, so he remained silent. Major Stone was dead, end of story. Sarah felt no guilt for liking it better that way.

"There's a larger pipe ahead," said Howard, stepping over a fly-tipped microwave. "You see it?"

Sarah did see it. This pipe had a circumference four times as wide. "The bus driver said the person in the ditch disappeared, right? Could have gone in here."

Howard nodded. "Let's be ready."

"Yeah, something killed that squirrel back there, so let's be extra cautious. It could be a stray dog or anything. The fight against crime is never ending."

"Glad to have you on the team." Howard pumped his first and smirked. She almost gave him back a smile in response. After a year of suffering her abrasiveness, Howard had finally learned to enjoy her bitter humour. She kind of hated him for that.

They trod carefully through the stagnant water until they stood in front of the large sewer opening. Despite her jokes, they both unholstered their guns. In the last year as an agent, Sarah learned something might try and kill you at any moment. That was what kept her awake at night. Along with the faces of the men she had killed.

Rusted bolts dotted the cement pipe's circumference, suggesting a grate once barred access. The midday sun shone inside only a few feet before impenetrable shadows took over. Warm, stinking air flowed outwards. Sarah felt the moisture settling on her face. She fought the desire to gag, muscles beneath her jaw tightened. "Smells like ass," she said. "We don't really need to go stomping around in here, do we?"

Howard raised an eyebrow and stuck out his angular chin. He was about to tell her off. "You want to abandon a lead?"

She sighed. "No, but I swear Palu is punishing us for something."

"You're paranoid. Come on, you said you want to get this over with, so let's look inside quickly."

"I can't believe I'm doing this." Sarah yanked the LED flashlight from the left epaulette of her black utility vest and clicked it on. The high-powered beam sliced through the darkness. The pipe was dirty: a place no person should enter voluntarily. Nonetheless, Sarah fixed the glowing flashlight inside her epaulette and started forward.

Their footsteps echoed as their boots splashed in the water inside the pipe.

Sarah wrinkled her nose as the stench assaulted her. "I really don't think we'll find anyone skulking around in here. Least of all, the Flower Man."

Howard apparently agreed, because in the glare of his own torch, his expression grew glum. "Shame, because I really want to catch that sicko."

Sicko is an understatement, thought Sarah. The serial killer the media had named the 'Flower Man' had killed twelve victims in just two months—a spree putting London's former murderous VIP—Jack the Ripper—to shame. This latest sociopath's MO was the stuff of nightmares. He made gardens from his victims—cutting out their eyes and stuffing the sockets with seeded soil and filling every orifice with aggressively growing plant life and insects. The harrowing part was that it worked. Victims became gardens, sometimes remaining alive for days with plants growing from their bodies. The last victim had been a twelve-year-old girl, discovered in a Lambeth ditch with daffodils growing out of her scooped eye sockets, and a dying Lupin planted inside an incision above her groin. Pain had sent the girl's mind to oblivion long before her body joined it, which took less than twenty-four hours after getting her to a hospital.

The details made Sarah sick.

Like Howard, she would love to get her hands on the Flower Man.

Yet, she also wanted to run away screaming. She was used to terrors by now, but the constant stream of abhorrent monsters the MCU faced was too much to bare. She had faced demons in the deserts of Afghanistan, but what altered her outlook forever was learning there were demons at home. Nowhere was safe, the United Kingdom: a glass palace built on sand. The thick scars on the left side of her face were a constant reminder of man's love of cruelty.

I just want to stop feeling this way.

As they delved deeper into the stinking sewer, plinks and plops surrounded them; condensation caused droplets to fall from the ceiling. The darkness ahead grew hot and muggy.

"I'm sweating," said Howard, swivelling his torch beam into an excited spiral as he reached up and wiped at his forehead.

Sarah nodded. "Me too. I've never been in a sewer before—I know, I know, what have I been doing with my life—but I'm not sure if this whole tropical climate-thing is normal. Is it?"

Howard shrugged. "Beats me. Sewer gases? I'm trained in underground ops, but I don't think this counts."

The deeper they went, the more Sarah was sure the heat was odd. Maybe it was trapped sewer gases as Howard suggested, but it still seemed out of place. Like walking through a greenhouse.

Howard stopped. "You hear that?"

Sarah stopped too. "I hear buzzing."

A corner lay up ahead, and despite herself, Sarah removed the safety from her gun. Without a word, Howard did the same. They both sensed it—something was wrong.

I always like something is wrong, thought Sarah.

She took a deep breath and crept around the corner, her gun raised. She batted at her face frantically. "What the fuck?"

Howard moved beside her and was also taken by surprise. He covered his face with the crook of his arm and ducked. "What is this? Flies?"

Flies were everywhere, but that wasn't what held Sarah's attention. In a wide cavern where the sewer opened into a nexus of separate channels, stood a tall lighting rig. Its warm orange glow, along with the droning buzz of its lamps, suggested it was ultraviolet. Weeds and plant life thrived all around.

"It's a garden," said Sarah.

It was bizarre to find vibrant foliage in a dank sewer, and it transformed the entire area into a creepy grotto. Creepy, because it meant the Flower Man had been there.

Or was still there.

Realising the same thing, Howard swept the cavern with his Ruger P95. He spoke urgently. "If this is one of the Flower Man's gardens, he was here as recently as yesterday. He might still be close by."

Sarah swallowed. Once again, she stood in the den of an amoral monster. Her entire life was filled with wicked men—Hesbani, Al-Sharir, Dr Krenshaw... her father. She felt sick to her stomach, as if the Flower Man had left behind a noxious ooze that she now inhaled. She wobbled and reached out, but there was nothing to hold on to, and she almost fell.

"Sarah, you okay?"

"Let's phone this in. I need some goddamn air."

Howard lowered his gun and moved towards her. "Hey, it's okay. It's just a bunch of weeds. I don't think he's here."

Sarah righted herself and stood straight. "It's a bunch of weeds growing in a stinking sewer, put there by a deranged psychopath who turns people into flowerbeds. Just standing in this place makes me..."

Howard frowned. "What?"

"I don't know." Vulnerable. "I just want to get back outside where I'm not breathing in piss and shit."

Howard reached out and squeezed her arm. "Okay. Let's get out of-"

"Hwah Mah!"

Howard spun and raised his Ruger. Sarah did the same with her SIG 229. The strange noise had come from a large patch of flowers growing beneath the heat lamp.

"Hwah!"

Sarah looked around, searching desperately. Then she saw something. "Oh God, no!" She stumbled over to the centre of the cavern and knelt beside a large flowerbed. Howard tried to move up beside her, but she pushed him away. She wanted an unobstructed view.

The girl was still alive.

"I'll call an ambulance," said Howard, seeing for himself what lay in the flowerbed. His voice thick, nauseous. He pulled out his mob-sat and dialled.

Sarah focused on the victim. The girl's age was indeterminate because of the wet mud and moss caking her face. Sensing Sarah beside her, she shook her head from side to side and mumbled urgently. She could form no words because wet dirt packed her mouth. A pair of rubber tubes ran down her nostrils, allowing her to breathe, and both her eyes had been scooped out and replaced with wilting daffodils. Sarah needed to help the girl.

But there is no helping this girl.

"It's okay, sweetheart," she said. "I've got you now. My name is Sarah. I'm a police officer."

The girl's mumbling became more frantic, suggesting she understood. Victims were often most manic when finally rescued.

Sometimes you had to stop them from injuring themselves in the panic. Relief could be even more powerful than fear.

In a panic of her own, Sarah clawed the dirt from the girl's mouth and removed thin root tendrils with her fingernails. Insects scuttled up her wrists. Whatever the Flower Man had planted had not yet sprouted, and with every finger-full of dirt gone, the girl spluttered and moaned a little more. Eventually, she gasped and choked, her throat clear for the first time in... how long?

"Mhwa Har. Mhwa Har."

Sarah stroked the girl's feverish brow. "Okay, sweetheart. Don't talk. Just stay calm."

"Shit," said Howard. "I can't get a call through down here. I need to go outside."

"Then go!" Sarah shouted at him.

"Heev fwear."

Sarah stroked the terrified blind girl's face. "It's okay, sweetheart. Help is coming. You're safe now."

The girl shook her head. "Nooo! H-h-heeeee heeeeere. He's heeere."

* * *

Sarah stumbled. Her SIG trembled in her hand and she almost dropped it.

Shit shit shit.

The blind girl's warning was clear. She mumbled it over and over: "He's here. He's here. He's here."

Howard shot an arm out to steady Sarah. "We don't know he's still here. He might have fled when the bus driver saw him."

"He's here. I know it."

Splish splash splish!

Footsteps came from the sewer tunnels.

A beast stalked the shadows.

Howard's hand still gripped Sarah, and for once, she didn't shrug him off. Everything about this felt wrong.

Splish splash splish!

"He's here! He's here!"

The blind girl's shouting jolted Sarah. She looked at Howard and pointed. "Take position!"

He gave no argument and hurried to the far side of the cavern, dissolving expertly against the wall. Sarah stayed with the victim, SIG no longer trembling, finger poised over the trigger.

The blind girl screamed.

"What is all that noise?" came a high-pitched, yet stern voice from the tunnels. "A garden is a quiet place. We'll have no noise. You are... Hmm, yes... oh my..."

The blind girl thrashed and squealed like a stuck pig at the sound of the voice.

What monster can do this to a person? thought Sarah.

The wet footsteps in the tunnel had halted.

The killer knew they were there.

Sarah and Howard peered at one another, jaws tense, eyes wide.

Help me! the victim begged. Don't let him get me.

"Quiet," shushed Sarah.

The footsteps in the tunnel retreated. Quickly. The killer was running. The blind girl's mouth had been packed with soil, but now she screamed. Her pleading had given them away.

Sarah raced out of the floodlit cavern and sprinted into the dark sewer tunnel, but was halted as she stumbled into knee-deep water. She had to battle to keep from falling under. "MCU, stop... stop right now!"

Ahead, a shadowy figure tilted around a corner. The Flower Man had got a head start on her. Sarah took aim and fired, hoping to scare him into stopping, but it didn't work. The Flower Man was getting away.

"Sarah!" Howard appeared to her left, at waist height and clear of the water. He reached down. "Get out of the muck. There's a walkway up here."

Sarah grabbed Howard's hand and hoisted herself up. Atop the walkway, the two of the them sprinted side-by-side. Sarah was the faster runner of the two, but her waterlogged boots slowed her down. As such, they rounded the corner at the same time and were met by a long, high-ceilinged tunnel. The Flower Man had not got far enough ahead to escape pursuit. In fact, they were gaining on him.

"He's slow," said Howard, sweating from the heat they'd left back in the cavern. "We're catching up to him."

Sarah increased her pace. Her flesh squirmed—she was about to come face to face with a monster—but the girl's screams echoing through the tunnel behind her was enough to spur her onwards. "MCU!" she hollered. "Last chance. Stop now or I will fucking kill you!"

The suspect kept running—in a strange, limping gait—and didn't look back. Sarah and Howard continued gaining on him, and he was no longer a silhouette. His features had taken shape. Tall. Skinny. With a lame left leg.

"Stop!" Howard ordered. "It's over."

It's over. Sarah repeated the words in her head, enjoying them.

The Flower Man's reign of terror was about to end.

Another monster removed from people's nightmares.

Is that why she still did this, why she still chased bad guys? Would catching this monster allow her to sleep tonight?

She doubted it.

When they reached the next corner, the Flower Man had disappeared.

Howard looked around urgently. "Shit, where did he go?"

Sarah slowed her sprint to a jog and switched her tact from speed to caution. The sewers were a maze—a labyrinth—and the Minotaur lurked.

"Eyes open, Howard. He's hiding."

Howard and Sarah fanned out, Howard dropping back, Sarah taking point. Ahead, the walkway widened as the sewer channel entered a closed pipe underneath. Sarah waited for Howard to catch up, and they fanned out again, moving to opposite sides of the cavern. The smell was foul. Sarah's wet boots slid over the slime coating the ground. This deep in the dark, she feared she might never see the light again. The beam of her torch seemed to get smaller, but it had to be in her mind.

Howard gave a silent signal with his fingers, motioning ahead. There.

Sarah saw it and nodded. Up ahead lay an open doorway, a sheet of metal hanging on a pair of hinges. "Might be his office," said Sarah, her sarcasm lacking its usual passion. The cries of the blind girl had faded, but they still echoed in Sarah's head. They abandoned her to give chase; failure was not an option. The room ahead was dark, a black cube daring them to enter. Sarah went inside.

Howard grabbed her. "I'll take point."

Sarah let Howard move through the doorway and gave him a few steps before following. There was once a time when her nerves were gilded steel, but after having to shoot her own father, who had just massacred half of Parliament, her courage had run dry. That was why she trembled all over.

Their flashlights lit up the new room, exposing it for what it was. The floor held a grimy mattress. Crates of bottled water lined one wall. It was a bedroom. The sewer wasn't just the Flower Man's killing ground; it was where he lived.

The newspapers enjoyed speculating about whether London's worst serial killer had a family—kids and a wife—as many killers did, but it was clear now that this monster possessed no humanity at all. No more than a sewer rat.

"Jesus." Howard pulled a face. "He sleeps here."

Sarah threw out a hand. "Howard, look out!"

Howard was caught by surprise. A length of wood cut through the shadows and clocked him right in the chin. He grabbed his face and crumpled to the ground. He still clutched his Ruger, but was in no state to take a shot. Sarah brought her own weapon to bear, but the Flower Man dropped the length of wood and pounced on her. The back of her head collided with the brick wall. Stars danced in front of her.

Despite his lame leg, the scrawny man wearing gardener's overalls was deceptively strong. He punched Sarah and crushed her nose, blinding her with tears. As she bent over, clutching her face, her attacker elbowed her in the ribs hard enough to floor her. If not for the fact she had survived her fair share of beatings in the past, and had grown accustomed to them, she would probably have been out for the count. But her body had hardened in the last year. She bit back the pain and rolled back to her feet.

The Flower Man descended on her again, like an angry wasp, jabbing and batting at her. "You will not come here and spread your pollution," he yelled, his high-pitched voice echoing off the narrow walls.

Sarah chanced a kick, making contact with her attacker's lame leg. He bellowed in agony and backed off immediately.

Sarah reached to her belt and grabbed her cuffs. This might be her only chance to get the suspect under control, and she needed to end things now before things turned lethal. Flicking open the cuffs, she lunged forwards, attempting to secure the man's wrists before he had time to recover, but he reacted quickly enough to dodge away. Off balance due to her lunge, Sarah took the full brunt of an uppercut to the face. The Flower Man grabbed her by the throat and squeezed.

Sarah struggled, but the fingers around her throat were like tightening vines.

"Hey, Green Dick!"

The Flower Man turned in time to see that same wooden plank now swinging at his own face. He tried to duck, but the plank walloped his forehead, and he dropped to the ground.

Sarah gasped, sucking in air and choking.

Howard stood over her. He dropped the piece of wood and put a hand out to her. "You okay?"

"I had it," she said, shrugging him off and getting up on her own.

"No, we had it," said Howard, ignoring her anger as he always did.

Sarah grunted. She picked up her cuffs and strode towards the moaning serial killer. "Your gardening days are over, arsehole."

The entire room shook.

Howard tripped and fell into Sarah as the world continued rumbling. Both of them fell to the ground in a heap as stone chips rained from the ceiling. Even with their flashlights, it became impossible to see through the dust cloud filling the room.

Somewhere far off, a distant dragon roared.

Sarah reached out and found Howard in the chaos. Their hands met and locked together. "What the hell is happening?"

"I-I don't know. An explosion?"

Sarah shielded her face and clambered to her knees. "We need to get out of here before the roof comes down. We have to get back to that girl."

Howard braced himself against the wall and started to climb. The room had stopped shaking, and the dust was clearing. His left eye had swollen shut where the Flower Man smacked him with the piece of wood. "Let's get sewer man cuffed and secured. Then we'll call for help."

Sarah nodded. She still clutched the cuffs and was unwilling to waste another second. Whatever just happened was secondary to the fact that they had a mission to complete. It might be her final mission, so she was going to make it count. The Flower Man was going to rot in a jail cell because of her.

She had him.

He was down.

Finished.

Sarah stared at the empty space on the ground and cursed a dozen times. In the confusion, in the disarray...

The Flower Man had escaped.

"He's gone," said Sarah. "I let him get away."

Howard stood beside her. "We let him get away."

Chapter 2

Sarah stayed with the girl until help arrived, which consisted of a single ambulance. She would have expected a greater response for a victim of the Flower Man, but other things were going on, apparently.

Howard stood beside Sarah, talking to Palu on the mob-sat. Sarah had wanted to remain inside the sewer with the victim, but needed to get out of the place. The smell... The damp... Like being in Hell. That she had let the Flower Man escape was enough to make her tear her hair out, but instead, she clenched her fists and remained silent. Brooding. She sat down on the grassy embankment and waited for Howard to finish his call. When he ended it, he stared at her.

"What is it?" she asked, already knowing it was bad. The explosion in the sewer had felt like the end of the world.

Howard shook his head like he couldn't believe what he was saying. "Tower Bridge... it's gone."

"What do you mean, gone?"

Howard stared off into the distance, his voice weak when he spoke. "I mean, it's gone, Sarah. Shit, this insanity never ends. You think you're making a dent—that there's just a certain allocation of evil in the world, and that every victory brings you a little closer to ending it altogether—but it's not true, is it? Evil never runs out."

"Howard, tell me what happened."

He shook his head as if snapping out of a daze. "Sorry. Palu told me that a group of suicide bombers walked into the centre of Tower Bridge thirty minutes ago, and blew themselves up, with enough force to sink the entire structure. While we were trying to bring down one psychopath, a whole group of them were sneaking up behind us."

Sarah didn't have it in her to offer words of solace to her partner, who seemed like he needed them. There was no solace to be had. Howard was right—evil never ran out. It was that conclusion which led Sarah to want out of the MCU as soon as possible.

Howard sighed. "We need to go. Palu wants us at the scene before the police screw things up."

Sarah glanced over at the sewer pipe. The one that led to Hell. "What about the girl?"

"Nothing we can do for her now. Palu is trying to get a couple of uniforms to secure the site, but for now, we need to leave her with the paramedics."

Sarah reached up and touched the scars covering the left side of her face. "She would have been better off dead. She'll never heal from this."

"Least we gave her a chance to try."

Sarah turned and climbed up the embankment. Because of them, the Flower Man was still at large, free to destroy more lives. They had got their shot and wasted it. Who knew if they would get another.

They both headed back to the car in silence. It wasn't until they reached the jet-black Range Rover parked at the side of the road that the silence was broken.

Sirens.

Ambulances raced past, but were uninterested in the girl in the sewer. They were heading to Tower Bridge.

Or where Tower Bridge used to be.

Sarah slid into the passenger seat. "Let's go," she said. "Let's just go."

* * *

If not for their Range Rover's sirens and flashing lights, Howard and Sarah would never have made it to the scene of the explosion. London's veins were clogged with fleeing traffic, but multiple emergency vehicles headed in the other direction. Howard's driving was advanced enough he rolled over the pavement and across verges when needed, but even then, they took an hour to drive four miles.

Howard parked in the middle of the Horsleydown Lane. The Range Rover didn't block access as the road had been cordoned off. When she got out of the car, Sarah witnessed a perverted postcard—an iconic London structure beneath a clear blue sky, spanning the Thames—distorted by billowing smoke and raging fires. Cables and ironwork twisted into the air above chunks of disembodied road that jutted out from both sides of the river. A yacht bobbed in the river, capsized amongst the debris—its dead occupants were being fished out by a pair of police officers in a speedboat. A crowd of thousands huddled around the embankments on both sides of the Thames.

A Met officer strolled up to meet Howard and Sarah as they approached the cordon. "Do you have business here?" he asked.

"Just sightseeing," said Sarah. "Would you take a picture for us?"

Howard touched her arm, signalling her to let him do the talking. "Officers Hopkins and Stone from the MCU. We're part of the first response team."

The officer nodded, but asked for ID. Howard showed his, but Sarah never bothered with hers. Luckily, one set of credentials was enough, and the officer lifted the cordon and allowed them to crouch beneath it. On the other side, Sarah and Howard sidestepped a row of body bags. A cursory glance tallied at least a dozen victims. More casualties floated in the Thames—various corpses missing arms, legs, and faces.

Human flotsam.

"This is bad," said Howard, staring at the river where the two hundred-foot bridge once stood. Both of its towers had fallen forwards into the water. "We dropped the ball."

"This isn't our fault," snapped Sarah, although she was thinking the same thing. How had they not caught this? The MCU had more funding and resources than ever, and they had been on a roll. First Hesbani, then Krenshaw and Major Stone. The wins kept on coming.

But this loss was enough to erase every win.

Tower Bridge... Gone.

Howard shuffled beside the river like a zombie, staring out at the flaming debris. Like Sarah, this last year had taken a toll on him. He was less brash than he'd used to be, not quite so cocky. Although she hated to admit it, Sarah liked him more with the extra weight he now carried—they had a connection grounded by mutual loss.

Sarah grabbed a police officer and asked for a briefing. The stern, older woman grunted, but reeled off the details: Four suicide bombers with a hostage made a speech, then blew themselves up in the middle of the lunchtime rush-hour. A hundred dead at least. Howard and Sarah got into the groove, speaking with witnesses and searching for clues. Hard to believe they'd spent the morning chasing a serial killer only to be met by this.

Chaos.

An hour passed, but they learned little of use, which was why Sarah was relieved when a black Range Rover arrived and parked next to theirs. She was less relieved when it was Thomas who stepped out of the car.

That's all I need.

Howard sensed her distraction because he hurried over to her side. She nodded to him that she was okay. Thomas was joined by Mandy, expressionless as usual, despite the scene of devastation meeting him. Thomas, on the other hand, was all emotion as he passed by the cordon with his hands buried in his thick blond hair. "The bastards," he said in his strange mix of British and Floridian. "Sarah, are you okay?"

She frowned. "I'm fine. The people on the bridge are less well."

He nodded, looking around with wide eyes. "I can't believe this. What is wrong with this world? When does it end?"

"Been asking that ourselves," said Howard.

Thomas ignored him and focused on Sarah. He motioned at her collar, which she realised was stained with blood from her nose. "I heard about the sewer tunnels. Are you hurt?"

"How's the victim?" asked Sarah. "How is the girl?"

"In the best care," said Thomas, "but she's pretty messed up. Too bad we let the bastard get away."

"I let him get away," corrected Sarah. "I had him."

Howard touched her arm. "You're not to blame, Sarah. The explosion..."

"Hopkins is right," Hopkins was right. "The Flower Man is on the run now. It's just a matter of time until he's apprehended. We'll address that issue later. Right now, we need to respond to what we have here."

Sarah folded her arms. "Do we have anything from above?"

"Plenty. Mandy, find somewhere we can set up."

They made their way to a cafe at the edge of the blast site. The windows had shattered, but no one inside was injured. The owner kept free coffee on the go for everyone present and the place was full of investigators and reporters. Mandy found a quiet corner by the kitchen and set down a laptop he'd been carrying in a holdall. Mandy was a man of few words, so gave no introduction to the video he opened on the screen.

"Taken from a cell phone," Thomas explained, but then corrected himself. "A mobile phone."

"It's okay, we speak American as well as you speak English," said Sarah, not looking her estranged husband in the eyes. In fact, she hadn't looked him in the eyes since he'd returned from the dead a month ago. She had done her utmost to avoid him. She needed time to think.

Maybe a lifetime.

The video played in high quality, taken on a top-spec camera phone. What it lacked was proximity. The spectator had wisely kept their distance from the bridge, and the footage seemed to come from a second-storey window. It showed four men standing in the centre of Tower Bridge, possibly of Middle-Eastern descent. A blindfolded woman struggled on her knees in front of them, fighting to get away but held down by rough hands.

"Who's the hostage?" asked Sarah.

"Maxine White," said Thomas. "UKIP MP for Hendon."

"Any reason she would be targeted?"

"Plenty. She's pretty much the poster child for increasing war efforts in Syria. She's a hardliner for eradicating ISIS through whatever means necessary, including high-yield missiles. There's rumblings she's also been trying to follow France's lead by banning the burka. Farage has been grooming her as his successor and she's been gaining support."

"She might as well have painted a target on her forehead," said Howard. "Anti-Muslim... Right-wing... Misguided."

Sarah winced as the video footage flickered and distorted, a massive blast of light blooming in the middle-ground. The bridge came apart like a bundle of crisp leaves, and a second later the laptop speakers squealed with distortion. The video ended with the spectator taking cover as stone and metal rained down on the Thames.

Sarah chewed a knuckle. When she removed it, she tasted blood in her mouth. "Whatever Maxine White believed in, she didn't deserve this. We need to find out who is responsible."

"We already know," said Thomas.

* * *

"It was Shab Bekhier," said Thomas.

Sarah recoiled. "What?"

Howard frowned. "Shab Bekhier disbanded after we took out Hesbani."

"Hesbani never controlled Shab Bekhier," said Sarah. "Al-Sharir does."

"Sarah..." he looked at her. "Al-Sharir is dead. He hasn't been on anybody's radar for years."

"It's true," said Thomas. "I spent five years in the desert amongst a dozen different terrorist cells, and by the time I came out of cover, I had stopped hearing Al-Sharir's name all together."

Sarah gritted her teeth. "Five years is a long time."

Thomas sighed. "Sarah..."

"Thomas!"

"I went undercover to try and prevent things like this from happening. My life seemed like a small price to—"

"We have more footage," Mandy interrupted, breaking the tension before it had a chance to grow. He spoke so rarely that, when he did, it made people stop and pay attention. They turned back to the laptop, and he played another video.

Again, Thomas gave introduction. "The previous footage was submitted to our website by an anonymous witness. This, however, was taken from a news chopper. From the look of it, the terrorists were waiting for the media to arrive, because when they spotted the helicopter, they began their speech. God bless the news crew for having a parabolic mic mounted underneath their bird. They captured it all."

The audio was muffled, like someone talking with a plastic bag over their head—and the screams from the bridge didn't help matters—but Sarah could fill in most of the blanks from context. One of the four bombers stepped forward and opened his arms revealing a torso strapped with chemicals and wires. Some kind of nitro bomb, Sarah suspected. The man stared up at the helicopter as he spoke.

Today we lay waste to your nation as you lay waste to ours. We fight for freedom, rejecting tyranny. Your false idols of security and power fail you. Shab Bekhier will show you the way. Shab Bekhier will lead the world to a new day—a day of truth and enlightenment. This is your warning, heathens. Praise be to Allah.

Once again, Sarah flinched as Tower Bridge exploded. This time, though, she found her anger. "If this is Shab Bekhier, Al-Sharir is behind it. Only he could pull off something so big—so evil."

"We don't know that," said Howard. "Hesbani was behind the last attack we thought was Al-Sharir. This could be another former Lieutenant of Shab Bekhier, or someone using their name."

"Al-Sharir had no other Lieutenants," said Sarah. "Hesbani is dead, so this has to be Al-Sharir."

Thomas reached out to touch her, but she took a step back. He appeared hurt by the reaction, but she didn't care. He exhaled. "Sarah,

Al-Sharir is gone. If I learned anything in the desert, it's that."

She wasn't listening. Her hand drifted to her belly where once she'd held a child—her and Thomas's child. Life had been heading in a drastically different direction before she crossed paths with an evil man in the deserts of Afghanistan. Hesbani may have taken her face, but Al-Sharir had taken her life. He wasn't gone like Thomas naively assured her. She felt him. Her skin crawling every time she whispered his name. He was still alive.

Waiting for the time to strike.

Hesbani had done unfathomable damage to the United Kingdom during his attacks, but this felt worse. A London landmark gone in an instant.

What next?

Howard saw Sarah panicking and made eye contact with her as he spoke. "Sarah, listen to me. We'll put a stop to whatever this is, I promise."

She focused on his soft brown eyes, finding a modicum of calmness in the way they gazed at her. "I just need a minute," she said. "Give me a minute."

Howard stepped back. "Okay."

Sarah turned away and started walking.

"Sarah," Thomas called out, but she ignored him and headed for the door.

Outside, the devastation hit her all over again. More body bags had piled up, and shocked victims woke from their stupors and began to weep and moan. Sarah kept her distance, not wanting to stray too near to death. Her soul was tarnished by the evil acts of men like Hesbani. She worried what would happen if she absorbed more misery. Yet, misery came to her in a flood as her mind spun webs of rotting, sinewy despair.

Is Al-Sharir behind this?

Is he alive? Is he here?

Enough.

Enough of this.

The MCU had dragged Sarah into its world to help stop Hesbani—and she had done that. Job done. She had stayed too long, and it had made her sick. Now she wanted out. No more bombs. No more diseases or hostage situations. No more serial killers. And most of all, no more husbands returning from the dead. Sarah just wanted to be left alone, to hide away with her shattered mind and ghastly face. She was a soul destined for solitude, and it was time to admit that. In her pocket rested her mob-sat. One call to Palu and she could end this misery, remove herself from the never-ending nightmare. She could resign. The bad guys might never stop, but that didn't mean she had to keep on going.

She was done.

Like a weight had lifted from her chest, Sarah breathed deeply. Her steps felt lighter. Knowing she was finished, making the decision in her head, cleared away a black cloud that had been hanging over her for too long. She glanced back at the cafe where her colleagues—soon to be former—still huddled in conference, and experienced a slight twinge of sadness. She would miss Mandy and his strange ways. Would miss Dr Bennet and her unwarranted curtness. Howard, most of all, she would miss as a friend. They had become close, and that was precious to her—but not precious enough to keep living each day in terror. Realising you weren't as tough as you thought was unpleasant, but it was also strangely liberating. She was an aged boxer stepping out of the ring.

Beyond the cordon, the crowds had begun to thin, police finally gaining control over the scene. Many spectators wandered away once they realised seeing dead bodies wasn't as entertaining as they'd presumed. Gawkers were often unwittingly affected by the very horrors they were so eager to see, and would regularly turn away with stricken looks on their faces that Sarah always thought served them right. The growing gaps in the crowd allowed her to see that someone was watching her.

She frowned and stared back.

It took a moment to register who was watching her.

Then it struck her. The Flower Man.

"You son-of-a-bitch!" Sarah took off like a missile. The Flower Man bolted too, shoving aside a couple of teenagers and fleeing into the streets. A police officer stepped in Sarah's way, and she thrust a shoulder out and knocked him aside like a skittle. No way was she letting the Flower Man escape again.

I'll shoot him if I have to.

The Flower Man threaded through a row of parked cars and headed into an alleyway between a Polish supermarket and a pet shop. Sarah kept right on his tail, knowing she should call backup, but worried it might slow her down and allow the killer to slip away again. No way was that happening.

She pictured the girl in the sewer.

Screaming and blind—forever changed.

The Flower Man's limp was no match for Sarah's piston-like legs. She was a machine, fuelled by anger and a desire for violence. The killer was a fool for having followed her. He knew it, too, because he kept glancing back over his shoulder anxiously.

Why had he been watching her? Were serial killers really so arrogant? Well, the Flower Man's hubris was about to get him caught.

The chase moved into another alleyway behind a row of shops. The back yards were empty. Nobody was around. A chain-link fence punctuated the end of the road. A dead end.

Sarah gritted her teeth and picked up speed. Nowhere left to run.

The Flower Man sprawled against the fence and shook it wildly like a caged animal. Sarah slowed and approached him cautiously with her hand on her SIG. "Stupid, stupid, stupid," she mocked. "Why on earth would you tail the very agents who almost had you in a jail cell this morning?"

The Flower Man stopped shaking the fence and turned to her. He panted heavily, yet somehow managed to look smug. His dark, brown eyes seemed disembodied from his face, as though floating slightly out of their bony sockets. "Your face, it interests me," he said, staring at her scars as though they were a museum painting. "A wasteland beside a meadow."

Sarah scowled. "Trust me, I'm all wasteland. Right now, I'm about to lay waste to you."

He seemed not to hear her. "I wonder what could grow in a wasteland. What seeds might one sow? Your face could be a wonder."

"Down on the ground," Sarah demanded.

"You're tough. Hardy. I could keep you alive for years under the right conditions."

Sarah pulled out her gun. "Ironic, because I will make sure you spend the next fifty years alive in a prison cell under very bad conditions. Now, get on the ground before I shoot your goddamn cock off."

To her relief, the Flower Man raised his hands above his head and lowered to his knees. "I look forward to getting to know you, Agent."

"You'll get plenty of time, arsehole." She strode forward, skin tingling at the proximity to the killer but ready to take him down. She'd encountered evil many times before, but this man was not killing for a cause or a vendetta—not involved in any war, or fuelled by anger or loss, defiance or hate. No, this creature lacked emotion altogether. His face was a blank canvas stretched across a horde of writhing insects. Dark eyes that never stopped assessing.

Sarah stood in front of the kneeling man and reached around her back to grab her cuffs. "One move and I'll put a hole in you."

Her fingers grasped at air. Damn it.

Her cuffs were gone, likely still in the sewer where she had last tried to use them.

"Problem, Agent?"

"Just get down on the ground. Face down. Now!"

The roar of a vehicle entered the alleyway behind them and Sarah couldn't help but glance back and see it. A white van careened towards her, a lone man behind the wheel.

What the Hell?

In that split-second Sarah took her eye of the Flower Man, he leapt up, crashing into her and knocking her gun aside. Sarah tumbled backwards but didn't fall. She tried to bring her gun back around, but the Flower Man was too quick and jabbed her in the mouth with a stiff punch. She rocked back on her heels.

The van skidded to a halt, narrowly avoiding Sarah. She caught her balance and turned, hoping for aid, and when the side panel of the van slid open and three men jumped out, she was relieved.

"I'm an MCU agent. I need help to arrest thi-"

The men grabbed her under the arms and around the neck, dragging her towards the van. She kicked and tried to escape, but she was overpowered and off-balance. In front of her, the Flower Man stood startled, disembodied eyes stretched wide. The three men shoved Sarah into the back of the van, hitting her in the head enough times to stop her struggling. She cried out for help as they shoved a hood over her head, but nobody came. The most terrifying thing of all was that the three men then headed back out of the van and grabbed the Flower Man. They shoved him alongside Sarah before closing the door. She could feel the warmth of the killer's body against hers.

Her abductors drove away.

Chapter 3

Howard squeezed the mob-sat almost hard enough to break it. "Damn it, Sarah, answer the call."

"You should have stuck with her, Hopkins," said Thomas

"I'm not her babysitter. She said she needed a minute, so I gave her one. What should I have done, tied her to a chair? Not sure she would have appreciated that."

Thomas seethed. "She's struggling with the job, and you're her partner. You should have informed me."

Howard had known Thomas for only a month, but already he didn't like the man. The American assumed authority and treated everybody as a subordinate. Who did he think he was? Sure, he was Sarah's husband, which gave him reason to worry about her wellbeing, but where was that concern when he faked his death to go undercover in the desert? Howard was the one who had been by Sarah's side this last year, being a friend to her despite snarling opposition. Sarah was abrasive and rude, but underneath was something else he'd gradually been uncovering. The scars on her face were a mask that had started to slip.

But Thomas had screwed it all up.

Ever since he arrived at the MCU, Sarah's mask had reapplied itself firmer than ever.

"Why would she take off?" Thomas asked Howard, some of his anger gone and his tone more conciliatory. "Did she say anything to you about needing a break?"

Howard leaned back against the plate-glass window of the cafe. "She's burnt out, Tom."

Thomas bristled. Howard knew the American preferred to be addressed by his surname—Gellar—a habit from his days as an Army Ranger. "She's not burnt out, Hopkins. This last year has shown just how strong she is."

"This last year almost broke her," said Howard. "The man who disfigured her in Afghanistan popped up and tried to assassinate the Queen, and then her father tried to wipe out the Government. To top it all off with a nice little bow, her husband came back from the dead to say hi. She's burnt out, trust me. I've been seeing it for a while, but it's not my place other than to have her back. If she took off, it's because she needed to. I'm sure she'll check back again soon."

Thomas scrutinized Howard with glaring blue eyes. "If you believe that, then why do you seem so worried, Hopkins? If you squeeze that mob-sat any harder your knuckles will pop."

Howard peered at his clenched fist and willed himself to loosen his grip. "Just because I'm sure she's okay, doesn't mean I'm not worried about her. She's my partner."

"And she's my wife, which is why you should have updated me if you had concerns about her mindset."

"You're my concern, Gellar. The reason Sarah is a mess is because of you."

Thomas clenched his fists. "Careful, Hopkins."

"Don't threaten me. You're the new guy around here, Tom. You're the one who turned up and complicated everything."

"Sounds like you wish I'd stayed dead."

Howard huffed. "Sounds like your guilt talking."

"You don't know a thing."

"I know you're an arsehole."

Thomas stepped forwards, chin out. Howard stood still, but his hands rose from his sides. Bring it on, Geller.

"You two!" Mandy came running. He'd taken himself off to sit in the car, but was now returning urgently. "I just got off the line with Palu. Sarah's mob-sat just went offline."

"She probably switched it off," said Thomas, sounding unsure.

Howard said, "No. The tracking module never switches off. If it's gone offline, it's because the mob-sat has been destroyed."

"Or tossed in the Thames," added Mandy. "Either way, it seems like Sarah might not be planning on reporting back."

Thomas rubbed his forehead. Howard disliked the man, but he couldn't deny he looked genuinely worried about Sarah. "Maybe she doesn't intend on coming back," he said.

"That's her choice," said Howard. He hoped it wasn't true.

"Or she's in trouble," said Mandy. Anxiety looked wrong on the big man, like seeing a trembling rhinoceros. "She's disappeared on us before, Howard, and she needed us. If this really is Al-Sharir... They have history."

Howard felt the blood flow out of his cheeks. The last time Sarah vanished from the face of the earth was because her father had kidnapped her. Now the man was dead, so what were the odds of something like that happening to her again? Slim? Impossible?

Howard couldn't stand by and do nothing. As much as he might imagine Sarah just taking off, he couldn't imagine her tossing her mob-sat and disappearing completely. She wouldn't do that to them. Not after all they'd been through together. She would at least say goodbye. To him at least. Wouldn't she?

Howard got to work. "Mandy, get back on the line to Palu. I want to know the last location we have for Sarah's mob-sat. We're not losing her again."

***

Sarah winced as her ribs hit the unforgiving back of a wooden chair. Her captors immediately tied her wrists behind her back before stepping away. Would they leave her in the dark with a hood over her head? Who was doing this? What did they want?

Her kidnappers yanked off her hood and made towards the door. It was too dim to make anything out other than their backs. It looked like they had her in a storage room, little larger than a cupboard. A flickering lightbulb swung overhead and gave off a brief scattering of light—enough to reveal that her chair was the only piece of furniture in the room. The only other source of light was a rectangular window pane above the door. The thin shaft of light highlighted thick dust in the air. Seeing it made Sarah cough and turn her head.

The door closed, and her kidnappers left her there alone.

Minutes passed, and they returned, shoving someone else into the room with her. Sarah squinted, adjusting her eyes, then blinked until she could make out who it was.

The Flower Man.

He wasn't tied to a chair like her, but instead, he lay unconscious on the ground. A patch of blood stained the side of his scalp and suggested he had not gone quietly. Neither had Sarah, but they had not bludgeoned her like that. Had they taken more care with her?

They'd taken several minutes before tossing him in with her. Had they tried speaking with him? Did they know he was the nation's most-wanted man? A twisted serial killer? Would they care?

The Flower Man stirred. From Sarah's vantage point, he did not seem like a monster. Gangly and unattractive, but nothing about him cried 'killer'. It was his eyes that showed his true nature, and right now they were closed.

Soon, he would be awake.

Sarah tried to pull her arms forward, but they were bound tightly to the back of the chair. The chair's legs were bolted to the floor. She wasn't about to stand up anytime soon, so she bit her lip and fought her restraints. Had someone kidnapped her just to leave her at the mercy of a serial killer? What was the point? Would they gain a thrill from returning later to find her strangled to death?

There had to be a greater purpose.

She'd been taken for a reason.

As the seconds ticked by, Sarah searched for inspiration. The floor was carpeted with cheap blue fabric tiles—some of them missing—and the paint on the walls was peeling. Plaster crumbled in several spots where shelving racks might once have stood. It was an abandoned building; Sarah was sure.

Trapped in an abandoned building with a serial killer.

Sure, why the hell not?

The Flower Man gasped and sat up.

Shit!

Sarah gritted her teeth and yanked at her bonds harder. The ropes tore at her wrists, but she felt them give a little. If they had been nylon or wire, she'd be screwed. She sawed her wrists back and forth, working at the knot millimetre by millimetre, as quickly as she could. Each minuscule gain brought agony as flesh shore away from her wrists. The Flower Man remained on the ground staring into space. He had not come-to yet and seemed confused about where he was.

Sarah struggled.

The ropes loosened.

Blood flowed down her wrists.

The Flower Man climbed to his knees, then to his feet.

He looked at Sarah. Saw her.

Shit shit shit.

Time had run out.

The Flower Man stared at her but didn't seem to understand. Then his eyes lit up, and a slippery smile stretched across his lips. "Meadow? I feared we'd been parted."

Sarah struggled. "Stay the fuck away from me!"

"Don't be so coarse." He slunk towards her, long arms and legs swaying like reeds.

"Get the fuck away from me!" she shouted louder, hoping someone would come help her. Wishful thinking.

The Flower Man leered over Sarah, his mouth smacking within inches of hers. Bizarrely, he gave off the scent of fresh cut grass. His teeth glinted pure-white in the dimly lit room. "Silence... petal."

Sarah's neck stiffened, and she struggled to breathe. The ruined side of her face throbbed as blood pumped through the brittle capillaries there. The monster standing over her reached into the pocket of his thick work-trousers. For one terrifying second, Sarah thought he was going for a knife, but then realised it was nothing so large. The Flower Man cupped something in his left hand, but his other seized her face, pressing down over her nose. Sarah grunted, and he shoved his left hand against her mouth, crushing the hidden contents against her mouth, scratching at her lips. She struggled, but the hand clamped over her face was like a Venus Fly Trap, and she couldn't take a breath.

Except through her mouth.

"A true gardener does not seek optimal conditions," the Flower Man whispered into her ear, "he seeks to create life in harsh, unwelcoming conditions. That is the true aim. Your face is barren, but I shall make it grow again—like a meadow."

The word 'barren' chilled Sarah, but she was powerless to fight back. Another second passed, and she could resist no longer. Her lips parted, and she gasped.

Along with air, she swallowed something else. Something bitter.

"Seeds, my petal. Blue Phacelia, the perfect flower for a desert like you."

Sarah gagged, spitting out seeds but choking on several that went down her throat. Her attacker was crazy. Did he expect a flowerbed to sprout suddenly from her ears? "You're insane."

"Some might say. The truth is I possess clarity most—if not all—lack. Do you not see the scourge set upon this world by mankind? Take this room for instance—a peeling, insect-laden pit. Unused, yet taking up a patch of land where nature might thrive. Mankind takes what it wants, and far more than it needs. We are spiralling towards our doom, Meadow, but I am fighting back. I fight for that which cannot defend itself."

"F-Flowers?"

"Nature. Everything that is not man, for man is a weed ruining the greatest and most beautiful of gardens."

"You kill innocent people for nonsense," said Sarah.

"No human being is innocent."

"You need help. Actually, right now, we both need help."

He smiled at her, took a brief glance to his left and right. "You're probably correct. I assume our hosts are interested in you and not me, but we shall see. We could have hours together until then—those men seem very busy. Plenty of time to tend to you."

Sarah struggled with her bonds again. "Leave me alone. Just... Please, don't!"

"Do not fear. We shall do this together."

He lunged forward, mouth against her neck and biting.

Agony.

Sarah screamed.

The Flower Man took out another handful of seeds and shoved them into the ragged wound he had opened above her left shoulder, grinding them down deep into her bleeding flesh.

Sarah screamed louder.

The Flower Man snarled and went to bite her again. This time, he aimed for the other side of her neck. Sarah's instincts took over, and she dropped her head, catching her attacker's mouth with her forehead. The Flower Man snarled and clutched his jaw—more angry than hurt. Sarah saw blood glisten over his teeth as he sneered at her. Did he enjoy the pain? The blood on his lips? Lifting a finger, he wagged it at her like a disapproving school teacher. "The sweetest roses have the sharpest thorns. You will be glorious in bloom."

He lunged at her again, just as the door behind him opened. The squeaking hinges distracted him, making him spin around. Sarah didn't get a clear view of what happened next, but there was a loud clonk, and the Flower Man fell at her feet. This time, a great deal of blood leaked from a wound on his forehead.

"My apologies," said her saviour. "I sought to arrive sooner. Pressing business matters, I'm afraid. I am sure you understand, Sarah. It is good to see you again."

A man stepped forward out of the shadows, entering the shaft of light coming from the glass panel above the door. Clean shaven and suited, he was a different person from the man Sarah had once known.

But it was still undeniably him.

Al-Sharir.

Chapter 4

Sarah's boogeyman stood before her in the flesh. Years of torment, of sleepless nights and panic attacks, all because of this man, swarmed through her brain, yet she could vocalise nothing. She shied away, a frightened girl. The thing she hated most.

Al-Sharir, on the other hand, seemed pleased to see her; a benign smile on his face like a father greeting his kids after returning from work. "Captain Stone, how fateful to be standing in the same room as you again. Allah enjoys playing games, no?"

Sarah's tongue felt thick in her mouth. "W-what are you doing here?"

"I think you know. Business brings me here. Speaking of which, I was impressed with how you foiled my protégé last year. Hesbani always was difficult to control—he allowed anger to drive him instead of justice. Justice is always proper, always constrained by right and wrong, but anger—unbridled—is unwieldy and prone to misuse. It is good to see you, Sarah. I often reflect upon our time together in the desert. You have no child, I take it? Did you lie to me all along?"

Al-Sharir had released Sarah from her captivity in Afghanistan only because she was pregnant. Did he know she had lost the child soon after, or did he think she had lied to save her own life?

"My baby died after what you and Hesbani did to me."

"I did nothing. You damaged yourself by entering a country that was not your own and seeking to impose your unwanted ideals on an innocent population. No British soldier injured in Afghanistan is an innocent victim. You accept your fates when you wage war."

"My unborn child was innocent!" said Sarah, thrashing against her bindings. "I was in your country to help!"

Al-Sharir looked at her with what appeared as genuine sympathy. "I am sorry for your loss, truly, however deserved they may be. In your mind, life has rewarded you unjustly. I can only imagine how you feel about that. Angry, I would assume."

"You ruined my life."

"You and your armies have ruined thousands."

"You're a monster."

"I am just a man, and you are just a woman."

Sarah had forgotten how much the man spoke in riddles. She struggled to stay calm. "Let me go, Al-Sharir."

"Perhaps. Perhaps I shall kill you instead. I released you into the desert to be a mother, to turn away from your wickedness and live a decent life—the life of a good woman. Then, last year, I learn of you interfering with Hesbani as part of the MCU— another corrupt agency designed to subdue my people."

"Hesbani killed hundreds of innocent people. He was going to shoot the Queen."

Al-Sharir gave part of a smile and nodded. "Audacious, yes. A child throwing a tantrum, I am sad to admit. He should never have turned away from me."

Sarah was surprised. "You don't agree with what he tried to do?"

"It lacked greater design, but he was defending Allah's will. It is his capture and execution that pains me. His rashness was his undoing and I can blame no one for that. But let us not talk of the departed any longer. You are very much alive, Sarah. Your tormenter too..." he nodded at the Flower Man who was moaning on the ground. His head wound glistened but didn't leak fresh blood. "Should I wake him up and leave you to resume your interaction?"

Sarah still tasted the bitter seeds at the back of her throat. "If your plan is to punish me by leaving me at the mercy of a psychopath, then just get it over with. I won't beg you."

"Ha! Dear Sarah, my plans go far beyond you. You are but a symptom of an immoral world."

"Immoral?"

Al-Sharir nodded slowly. "Nations of sheep who pay footballers millions while 3rd-World doctors operate without supplies. Governments who see war as business and peace as recession. The West is a plague, and it is spreading. I shall be the cure."

Sarah shook her head, tired of the same old argument. "You think your way is better? Sharia law, forced worship?"

"It is not Sharia law, it is Allah's law, but no man should worship unwillingly. That is the problem—man's will is being eroded by an empire of sin. Will you deny He who gave you life?"

"The man who gave me life is dead because I shot him."

"An act of courage without a doubt, but your true father is eternal."

In another time, Sarah might have continued the argument until she had vented her frustrations, but she wanted this over with. "Kill me, I don't care. Whatever you are going to do, just do it, but don't kid yourself that there's anyone up there keeping score. You're deluded, and I feel sorry for you."

Al-Sharir stepped out of the light and knelt before her so that his face was in line with hers. "You truly seek death, Sarah? The last time we met, you begged for life. At any cost, if I remember."

"I've changed."

"I see that. Okay, I shall conclude our discussion." He pulled a knife from a sheath he held in his hand—a slim knife, tapered like a small sword. "I took this from a Russian when I was fourteen years old. Many have tried to take my country from me, Sarah. You are just the latest."

Sarah's death had been inevitable. Ever since leaving the desert, she had known this day would come. Al-Sharir would finish his destruction of her. Part of her welcomed it. She could never heal from the wounds he had inflicted upon her—only fester.

Let it be now, she thought. Let it just be over.

Still, Sarah couldn't ignore her fear as the blade hovered closer, moving towards her chest; but it did not pierce her. Instead, Al-Sharir thrust at the gap between her ribs and her arm, sliding the knife beneath her armpit until it was behind her back. Sarah didn't understand what was happening, but then she felt the blade saw at her bindings.

He was letting her go.

Al-Sharir pulled the knife back and placed it on her knee where it balanced precariously. "A gift to you, my dear. This man on the floor is an abomination. A creature born of darkness. Kill him, as I would. Do Allah's work by extinguishing this evil, and I will allow you to go free, to serve Him by my side."

Sarah couldn't help herself and laughed. "Join you? Are you insane?"

Al-Sharir showed no sign of insincerity. If anything, he appeared hurt by her reaction. "Is it so crazy? You and I are bound, Sarah. Allah wishes our destinies entwined, and it is so. You are angry, as I once was. You want to stop the horrors of the world. So do I. But you are fighting on the wrong side. Does it not exhaust you?"

Sarah surprised herself by answering. "Yes."

Al-Sharir nodded knowingly. "The anger will not leave you unless you free yourself from it. You joined the MCU to find justice, but you will find none in its false causes. Join me and truly change the world, Sarah. Let us end the time of soldiers and bombs. Your child could have grown up in a different place. A place where she would not be forced into the desert to risk her life for a false notion of freedom. I do not enjoy violence, Sarah. I do not profit from it. Humanity does not profit from it. Help me bring peace to the world."

Sarah shook her head, but didn't laugh anymore. Al-Sharir was as compelling now as he had been in the desert. What was he planning? How many more must die to incite his version of change?

Was he truly trying to make the world a better place? Could he? Could anyone?

"Join me, Sarah, and live. I shall leave you alone with this man—this creature who has killed so many. A serial killer as you would put it. He would see you dead, so you must act before he has a chance to."

Sarah glanced at the Flower Man and thought about the girl in the sewer—blinded and mutilated like all the other victims. Did a creature such as this deserve the gentle treatment of the British justice system? Was Al-Sharir's way better?

Did she have a better idea?

Al-Sharir walked away, giving her one last cursory glance as he paused in the doorway. "You are unfinished business, Sarah. Whatever choice you make, I shall end our affairs today."

The door closed, and a bolt slid across.

Once again, Sarah was trapped in the dark with a killer.

* * *

Al-Sharir had sliced Sarah's bindings and left. The ropes no longer dug into her skin and were becoming looser.

From the floor, the Flower Man grunted. "Meadow? Are you still there, Meadow?"

Sarah scissored her wrists back and forth, working the ropes free little by little. Returning blood flow made her fingertips throb, which only made her movements clumsier.

"Meadow?" The Flower Man stretched the word out as though tasting it. "Meeeeadooooow..."

Sarah shifted her body to the side, gaining leverage to free her wrists. Almost free, but her extended movement caused the knife placed across her knee to tumble to the ground. She'd forgotten all about it, but now she needed it more than ever. "Damn it."

The Flower Man rose to his feet. As the recipient of several beatings today, he was resilient to say the least.

Sarah got one wrist free—

The Flower Man rubbed at his head, saw the blood on his fingertips and growled.

—then the other wrist.

The ropes fell away. Sarah's hands were free.

The Flower Man wasted no time and dove at her like a snarling dog. Sarah freed herself in time to throw herself forward and out of harm's way. She slipped from the chair and landed on her knees. The Flower Man collided with the chair.

Sarah scurried towards the knife on the floor. It lay only a few feet away.

If she could just reach it...

The Flower Man fell on top of Sarah, pinning her face down against the dirty carpet tiles. "Time I planted you, petal." He wrestled with her arms, trying to force them behind her back.

"Get off me!"

"Not until I plant my seed in you. You will be my greatest work."

Sarah fought to free her arms, gasping in pain as her shoulder sockets strained.

She was powerless—her attacker too strong.

Her entire life had been spent fighting—fighting to get her father's attention, fighting to make it in a man's Army, fighting to overcome her demons—but now she was just another victim. Like the girl in the sewer, or the innocent people who had been going about their business on Tower Bridge.

Or her unborn child.

Sarah's chin smacked against the floor clacking her teeth together, but her fighting renewed and she strained with everything she had. Managing to yank one of her arms free, she threw it out ahead of her, scrabbling at the carpet tiles. Her fingers found the knife and wrapped around the leather handle.

"Stop fighting." The Flower Man clutched at her belt, busying his hands. "You cannot stop nature."

Sarah twisted onto her side. Then she swung the knife. With his hands busy at her belt, the Flower Man left himself undefended. The knife plunged right towards his face.

Clonk!

Sarah used the blade's pommel and aimed at the Flower Man's left eye, thudding against hard socket. He yelped with pain and fell away like a scalded dog. Courage returning, Sarah rolled onto her stomach and clambered to her feet. Putting her entire bodyweight forwards, she tackled the Flower Man to the ground and straddled his chest, pinning his arms. She used the blade's pommel once more, bludgeoning the Flower Man across his face and splitting the taut flesh above his cheek. His mouth formed a pained 'O' as his arms flopped weakly at his sides. Sarah had him beat.

The power belonged to her.

The knife trembled in her hand, tip pointed up towards the ceiling.

She rotated her wrist until the blade pointed downward. The tip hovered over the Flower Man's panting chest. Sarah could end the sick bastard now and do the world a favour. No waiting for justice, no risk of escape. Instant closure for the victim's families.

Maybe Al-Sharir's way was right. It got quicker, better results.

The knife felt heavy in Sarah's hand.

It would be so easy to plunge it downwards. Just put her weight on it and pop...

Sarah tossed the blade aside, sickened.

There was no denying the relief in the Flower Man's bulging eyes.

"I won't play Al-Sharir's games," said Sarah. "The only way to end violence is to trust in the justice we have. You and I are getting out of here, and then I am placing you under arrest to stand trial and answer for your crimes, you sick fuck," she added.

The Flower Man grinned. "Looking forward to it, Meadow."

Sarah punched him in the mouth hard enough make his teeth rattle. "One wrong move and I'll break your neck. This is over for you, understand? If you plan on escaping, think again. Only reason I didn't bury that knife in your chest is because I don't want your blood on me. So prepare yourself to spend the rest of your life in a cell. The alternative is you stay here and die. The man who abducted us is dangerous—more dangerous than you—and he won't have any patience for your brand of lunatic. Get it?"

In a rare moment of lucidity, the Flower Man kept quiet and nodded.

Sarah got to her feet. "Good. There's a glass pane above the door big enough to get through. You are going to hoist me up so I can knock it through, then I'll unlock the door on the other side."

She allowed him to his feet. It looked like he'd gone several rounds with Ivan Drago, but he nodded willingly. "Sounds like a plan."

Sarah stared up at the panel above the door. It didn't look thick, but knocking it through might prove difficult and make noise. Once she got through, she needed to be quick. Like it or not, there was no option not to release the Flower Man. He was the only one with interests matching her own right now. He was a cold and calculating creature, but intelligent enough to realise his fate if he didn't escape with her.

The Flower Man wiped his palms against his overalls. "Ready, partner?"

The wooden chair Sarah had been tied to was bolted to the ground. She took a run up and kicked it, but needed another three attempts to eventually knock out one of the backrest struts. She picked up the fallen length of wood and batted it in her palm. "Now I'm ready. Make a step up for me."

The Flower Man stood in front of the door and laced his hands together. "Giddy up."

Sarah strode forward and hopped up into his clasped hands. He hoisted her with ease—long limbs easily capable of handling her weight. Without asking permission, Sarah stepped onto his shoulders and raised herself up higher. Although he mumbled with discomfort, he obliged and held her ankles for support. His fingers against her flesh made Sarah's skin crawl.

"Hold me still. I'm going to knock it out." She placed one hand against the door to steady herself and raised the chair strut in the other. She held it in the middle like a javelin and smashed the end against the centre of the glass panel. Rather than shattering, the pane popped out whole and tumbled to the other side.

Sarah clucked. "Well, that was easy."

"We make a good team," said the Flower Man, still holding her ankles.

Leaning forward, Sarah peered through the gap she had made. The corridor beyond was lit, but out of the two fluorescent strip bulbs only the far one worked, which left the near stretch of hallway dim. At least no one stood out there—not a single guard posted. Sarah knew it was too good to be true, but she had to take advantage while she could. She wedged her elbows against the window frame and tipped forwards, hanging halfway out the gap. The fit was tight and gave her little room to manoeuvre. Her only choice was a headfirst lunge to the floor—with fingers crossed she didn't break her neck.

It was better than hanging around waiting for Al-Sharir to return.

"Be ready," she called back to the serial killer clutching her ankles.

"I am ready."

Sarah heaved herself forwards through the gap.

And then she fell.

Throwing her arms out, she tried to land safely, but her head hit the floor, and her weight came down awkwardly on her left arm. She crumpled onto her back in a heap. The pain was immediate—a stinging jolt running all the way to her shoulder. There was no time to lie there recovering, though, so she quickly hopped to her feet. Briefly rubbing her shoulder, she flexed her arm to test it. That she could still move it was the best she could expect right now.

"Meadow, are you okay?"

Compassion from a serial killer.

Or concern for his ticket out, Sarah thought.

She looked at the locked door behind her and considered turning her back on the Flower Man. It was a dumb move to free him, but she wasn't willing to abandon him to Al-Sharir's men. He belonged to her now, and she would be the one deciding his fate. For all she knew, Al-Sharir might end up letting him go. A risk she couldn't take.

The lock on the door comprised of a simple bolt, and Sarah slid it across. The door swung open and revealed a smiling Flower Man. "Very honourable of you, Meadow. I assumed you would leave me to rot."

"Not here, not yet." She yanked him by his arm and started him down the hallway ahead of her. He was still beaten enough to remain subdued, but if he got wind of the fact that her shoulder was wrecked, he might risk pouncing on her again. She had to hide her bruises. Just to be sure, she bent down and picked up the wooden chair spoke.

They headed to the end of the corridor. It didn't take long until they heard a voice. The door to the next room was ajar, and Sarah moved up to peer inside. A single man occupied it—he was talking on a mobile phone. Was this the guard in charge of making sure Sarah didn't escape? If he was, she had lucked out, because he had allowed himself to become distracted. Al-Sharir obviously hadn't expected her to team up with the Flower Man, and without him there would have been no escape. She could hardly believe this herself.

Speaking of whom, the Flower Man crouched beside her, following her lead. From the smile on his face, he seemed to be enjoying himself, but he was also squinting as if concentrating. Sarah put a finger against her lips to make sure he remained quiet. He nodded, but then resumed his thoughtful squinting, studying the man in the room.

The guard was not what Sarah expected. He was a white man, not Middle-Eastern, and it sounded as if he was speaking Russian. The only thing that mattered was that he was alone and distracted.

Sarah would get no better opportunity, so she crept up behind the man. He was so embroiled in his conversation he failed to notice her presence. She brought the wooden chair spoke down on the back of his skull and dropped him. There was no need to hit him again.

"Nicely done," said the Flower Man, inspecting her work with an appreciative grin. "One hit and done."

"Not my first time." She checked on the guard and was glad to see he was still breathing. He had no gun or weapons of any kind, which was disappointing. All he had was a walkie talkie. His job had been to radio in if something happened. Maybe Al-Sharir didn't want anybody hurting Sarah except himself.

So far, the escape had been easy. Too easy.

"We don't know what we'll find in the next room," said Sarah. "So be ready to run. We can't be far outside of the city, so we need to get outside and flag down help."

"Or to the nearest sewer."

Sarah couldn't tell if he was joking or not. He looked a sorry state with his head caked in blood and his chest panting, but there was no mistaking the animalistic glint in his eyes—like he might blink sideways at any moment—a lizard dressed like a man. Insanity seemed to ooze off him.

The next room they entered was a reception area with an old three-seat sofa and two empty vending machines. There was another door on the opposite side, leaving them no choice of direction. It wasn't ideal, but Sarah wasted no time. The longer they took, the more likely another of Al-Sharir's men—or the man himself—noticed their escape. The new door was thankfully unlocked, and Sarah opened it cautiously. Her heart thudded in her chest.

Please let this be a way out, or at least some place with a panic room and phone.

Her wishful thinking let her down, and Sarah found herself inside a wide-open warehouse. A dozen dangerous-looking men stared at her.

Oh shit.

The Flower Man grunted. "I think they see us, Meadow."

Sarah nodded. "It's a possibility."

She glanced about quickly, taking in everything she could. The one side of the warehouse was open, with several loading bay shutters raised up on their rollers. A large white van stood parked just inside. In the middle of the warehouse, a large group of men surrounded Al-Sharir, who seemed surprised to see her loose, but also amused by it. He was the cat and she was the mouse, they both knew it. Only three men pulled out guns, but they all pointed at Sarah.

"Could someone direct me to the toilets, please?" said Sarah, hoping they didn't shoot her right then.

"Sarah, I underestimated you," said Al-Sharir, smiling at her warmly. "I assumed you'd try to escape, but I expected it to take you longer than ten minutes. Did you pull the chair beneath the window? I made sure it was bolted securely."

She shook her head and then nodded to the Flower Man. "I got my friend to give me a boost."

The Flower Man waved. "Nice to meet you all."

Al-Sharir kept his focus on Sarah. "Working with your enemies for a greater purpose. You think much like I do. Have you considered my offer of alliance?"

"I am nothing like you," Sarah spat. "You expected me to commit murder."

"No, I only hoped you would. To have you with me would have been most elegant, but I assume you are choosing option B, which puts us in an uncompromising opposition. I don't play kindly with my enemies, Sarah, I shall warn you now."

"You'll always be my enemy, Al-Sharir."

A brief standoff ensued, which surprised Sarah, for she had no leverage. Perhaps Al-Sharir was still deciding whether to kill her. The Flower Man edged away. Sarah would do the same if not for the fact she was locked in a staring contest with the monster from her nightmares. She had no idea what to do, or what was about to happen.

Another moment passed. Al-Sharir sighed, pulled out a gun, and started shooting.

Sarah ducked just in time and fell into a run. More shots rang out, forcing her to duck her head and run blindly. She made for the open side of the warehouse—the only chance for survival.

If she could just make it outside...

The only cover was the truck, so she sprinted towards it.

"Wait for me." The Flower Man raced after her, arms flapping above his head.

Chunks of cement floor bounced up at their feet and ricochets bounced off the walls. That Sarah hadn't been hit yet was a miracle. It would only take a few seconds more before a slug eventually caught her. Then she would bleed out on the floor with her perpetual tormentor standing over her.

She dove towards the van and scrambled up against the side. She'd made it! A few seconds of safety were now hers.

"Stop! Stop shooting." Al-Sharir shouted at his men and the shooting petered out. "Sarah?" he said. "Sarah, we can't escape each other. Why not give in now? All that pain you carry with you. It can end."

Sarah slumped against the side of the van. There was something about this day that wanted her dead, and dread clung to her like a mouldy shower curtain. She wanted out of this life, but it had its talons in her and wouldn't let go. Maybe she should just step out and let a bullet claim her.

It would be so easy.

But Al-Sharir had stopped his men from firing for now.

Sarah frowned. Why?

Al-Sharir's men didn't have a perfect line on her, but they could easily suppress her until they had her surrounded. So why weren't they firing?

Because I'm standing next to the van.

What is inside this van?

The Flower Man knelt beside Sarah clinging to her like glue. He had stopped smirking and looked shell-shocked. Oddly, she felt responsible for him. She clicked her fingers in front of his face and regained his focus. He nodded to let her know he was still present.

The two of them were still screwed though.

Silently, Sarah pointed at the van's side door then at the handle. The Flower Man frowned, but seemed to understand her instructions. He rose from his knees and yanked open the side panel, sliding the door across on its rail.

Sarah staggered away from what she saw inside the truck. "God no!"

The Flower Man shook his head, a look of abject horror on his face. "We have to stop this."

Sarah prodded him. "There's no time. We have to get out of here."

The Flower Man nodded and came back to reality—they were being shot at—and they hurried alongside the van until they were outside the warehouse.

They were nearly free.

The sun was about to lose its grip on the sky. It would be dark soon.

"Sarah, you can't stop me." Al-Sharir called after her. "Nobody will stop me. This world will change."

Sarah and the Flower Man escaped the warehouse, and without looking back, they raced across an empty courtyard towards the main road. There was no gate, only a barricade which they ducked under without slowing. The rush of traffic on the main road in either direction allowed them to disappear.

Al-Sharir did not follow. Sarah was safe.

But not for long.

No one would be safe for long.

***

Now that she was out of the warehouse, Sarah's body gave out. Her injured shoulder sagged, and her tired legs shuddered with every step. By the time she reached the end of the road, she probably resembled a weird imitation of Elvis. The Flower Man followed closely, and he too looked ready to drop. Good thing, too, because if he tried to run, she could do nothing to stop him.

They dodged evening traffic as they fled the warehouse and Sarah noted street names so she could call down hell upon Al-Sharir. If she could find a phone soon, he would have no time to escape. But every time she tried to flag a driver, she was ignored—people did not stop on busy London roads.

She needed to make that call.

What she had seen in that van...

An alleyway led between a closed tyre fitters and a vacant warehouse. It spat them out onto a busy high street, and Sarah almost cried with relief. Night had fallen, but pedestrians still hurried back and forth. Their chattering was music to her ears. Shops still traded—their lights switched on and doors open. Sarah considered grabbing someone for their mobile phone, but then she saw something even better outside a Chinese greengrocer.

"Come on!" she said, grabbing the floundering Flower Man and dragging him across the road. "Don't try to run, because you won't get ten yards in the state you're in. All I need is one good Samaritan."

He glared at her, defying her assessment of him. "I may be hurt, but I have strong roots."

"Perhaps, but that doesn't mean you didn't get your arse handed to you several times today. I don't think you can take another beating. So move it!"

The Flower Man clutched the back of his head tenderly as if remembering quite how beaten he was, then rolled his eyes in resignation. Without further argument, he accompanied Sarah to the other side of the street where she hurried over to the payphone she had seen—an old-fashioned red booth you rarely saw these days. Perhaps it was a sign. Inside its metal confines, Sarah immediately felt safer. The Flower Man held the door and leaned in beside her. In a stroke of fortune, it was one of the few pay phones in London not at all vandalized, and it gave a dial tone without pause. Sarah called the secret number that MCU agents could call in emergencies. It put her straight through to command, which in the last year had become a hive of ten-dozen operatives. She didn't recognise the woman who answered the call.

"It's Sarah Stone. Put me through to Palu."

"Yes, ma'am."

Three seconds later: "Sarah, it's Palu! Where are you?"

Sarah squeezed the phone, wavering body sagging against the side of the booth. "He's alive," she shouted into the receiver. "Palu, Al-Sharir is alive."

"What?"

"He has a bomb. A nuclear fucking bomb."

Palu's voice was grave. "Sarah, tell me exactly where you are."

Sarah turned to find a street name, but a glint of metal caught her eye. She glanced down to see a thin dagger in the Flower Man's hand—the blade Al-Sharir had given her back at the warehouse.

She thought she'd left it back in the room, but he must have grabbed it while they were on opposite sides of the door.

The thin blade slid into Sarah's guts before she could say anything. It felt cold. And yet it burned. The Flower Man whispered into her ear as she fell. "I'm sorry, but I have gardens to tend to. Goodbye Meadow."

Sarah slid down the side of the booth to the floor, clutching the hole in her stomach as it leaked blood. Nobody on the street noticed her inside, and the Flower Man closed the door and simply left.

Yet again, the day wanted Sarah to die.

This time she felt like it might win.

* * *

The heat in Afghanistan drove the men crazy, but Sarah kind of liked it. Hamish was a pale Scotsman—so he suffered worse—but Sergeant Miller, with his dark-black skin seemed to tolerate it as well as Sarah did. Right now, Sarah was enjoying a little alone time in Camp Bastian. The place was abuzz with activity, as usual, but she found that it was easy to ignore if she closed her eyes and focused on the sun's rays against her skin.

Four months ago, she had arrived in the country. It was her first real tour after Sandhurst, and prior to it she had only been on low-security attachments in Germany and Poland. It felt good to finally be out in the field, where she could finally do some good. That she had been distracted by a young US Army Ranger was something she was aware of, and trying to fight. Yet, she couldn't help thinking about Thomas.

He was a sergeant attached to the 75th and had arrived in the UK side of the vast military complex that comprised Camp Leatherneck and Bastian to gain assistance with a patrol he was making. Sarah had taken his Intel and offered a small detachment of men on behalf of her commanding officer. Thomas had thanked her with a bootlegged bottle of wine during an evening that had ended with her hands down his fatigues. She still blushed at the thought. It didn't seem like he had been out to take advantage though, and when he said he would be back to see her soon, he seemed to mean it. In fact, he seemed excited at the prospect.

Was that why Sarah had spent her two days off sunbathing in the centre of camp where she could be easily spotted.

She was acting like a teenager.

But it was the first time she had ever felt like this. Her entire life had been dedicated to a military education—almost inevitable with a father in the SAS—and she had wasted no time with youthful frivolities. Sure, she had her share of male interest, but as soon as they met her dad, they always decided she was more trouble than it was worth. So she stopped bothering with trying to make friends or lovers. There were more important things in life. Only now was she finally in a place where she felt grown up enough to relax and live a little life. Sure, she was in a war zone, but she was happy. It felt like she was where she was meant to be.

Helping the local population hadn't been as rewarding as she had expected, and many of the Afghanis seemed to resent her presence. She had fought through it best she could, and her squad had delivered food and supplies to countless children, and offered medical assistance to a dozen villages. Whether the people wanted to be helped or not, they were being given aid. Every day, this country grew closer and closer to liberation, and one day, democracy would rule. Not everyone supported Blair and Bush on the decision to enter Afghanistan, but Sarah felt that the results would eventually speak for themselves. This was the start of something great—a harmonious and peaceful Middle-East. Sarah was proud to be a part of it.

And she was excited about seeing Thomas again.

So where was he?

Please tell me he wasn't just a player—the hot American guy from the other camp. Is he spilling the beans to his pals right now?

Almost like a mirage, Sarah's eyes spotted movement on the edge of the rec area. A man appeared beyond the open-air weights gym, moving between glistening chests and bulging biceps. He seemed to shimmer in his olive-green fatigues, but Sarah knew it was just the heat rising off the sand. Before Thomas came into full view, she had already known it was him. She had been sure.

He's here. Gosh, why is my stomach fluttering?

He spotted her sunbathing and frowned. "Hey, it's er... Sharon, right?"

Oh my God. Are you kidding me?

She leapt up from her chair. "Sarah!"

"Thomas. Pleased to meet you."

Sarah felt sick. She stared at the man and didn't know whether to punch him or kick him in the nuts. She might do both.

Thomas burst out laughing. "Your face is a picture. It's also extremely beautiful. Have you always been so perfect?"

Still off-kilter, Sarah wobbled. "Y-you're pulling my leg?"

"Yeah, I'm yanking your chain. I came here to see you, like I said I would. Haven't had a chance until now; you know how it is with the war and stuff."

She chuckled. "Yeah, it's a bother, isn't it?"

"You free today, or do you have orders to sit here?"

"I was... waiting for you," she admitted, then chastised herself for laying herself out so openly. She'd had such a closed-off upbringing, with only the distinguished Major Stone as a parent, but she had somehow ended up as an over-sharer. Often she would speak openly of her feelings and make people uncomfortable.

"So you are free?"

Sarah blinked. "Huh? Oh, yes. I'm free. How long do you need me for?"

"Why, do I need to sign a form or something? Let's start with lunch and see where it leads us."

"To dinner usually," she said. Wow, what a lame joke.

"And then to supper. May I?" He offered his elbow. Sarah took it, and together, the two of them walked through the military camp in the centre of the desert like a married couple.

Perhaps one day they would be, thought Sarah, then told herself to stop being such a silly girl. She was an officer of the British Army, not a teenager.

Still, maybe he's the one...

Maybe.

Chapter 5

Down in the depths of MCU's subterranean base, the Earthworm, Howard's mouth was dry, and he lugged a rotten carcass in his guts. He'd failed her. Again. Maybe it was unwise to care so much for a fellow agent—death was an ever-looming part of the job after all—but it was he who had recruited Sarah.

That made it his responsibility to keep her safe.

Good job, Howard. Really, great job.

The rest of MCU's senior team sat around the conference desk, looking equally sick to their stomachs. Sarah meant a lot to them all. They meant a lot to each other. You couldn't survive hell without company.

"How did we let this happen?" Thomas demanded.

"This isn't on you, Thomas," said Palu, pasty and white. "You just got here. This is my team. My mistake."

Howard nodded. "We're all in this together."

Mandy didn't speak, but he also nodded without hesitation.

Thomas just sighed. "We need to find her."

"It's been twenty-four hours, and we have nothing," said Palu, lacing his hands together in front of him and blowing out air. "How can terrorists blow up a London landmark and leave us nothing? How is one of our agents gutted in the street with no one seeing? This is not what the MCU is about. We do not fail; we do not fuck up. We are the angels that haunt the dreams of bad men. But today..." he shook his head with disgust. "Today we are broken and beaten. I don't understand how this happened."

Howard sighed. "It happened because Al-Sharir is supposed to be dead. Every scrap of intelligence coming out of the Middle-East tells us he has been missing for years."

Palu shrugged, looked angry even though Howard had said nothing to offend. "So what are you saying? Sarah's last words were untrue?"

"No! Sarah said she saw him, and I believe her. She was abducted and escaped—like she always does—but only after seeing something."

Thomas raised his eyebrows. "A nuclear bomb?"

"That's what she said. Why doubt her?"

"Because she has never seen a nuclear bomb up close, nor have any of us, I would imagine."

Howard looked away and grunted. "Perhaps it said Nuclear Bomb on the side, Tom, I don't know."

Thomas sneered. "Things need to be that clear for you to do your job, don't they, Hopkins? You are Sarah's partner. How many times has she been hurt, abducted, or threatened in that time? You're not fit for this job. You should step down—join the police."

Palu smashed his fist on the table and stared at Thomas. "Agent Hopkins is a damn fine agent and deserves better than to be spoken to in that way. And I would also inform you that being a police officer in this country is not a lesser calling."

Thomas sighed. "You're right. I apologise, Howard. I'm sure you did your best."

"My best? Gee, thanks."

"Enough, Howard," warned Palu.

Howard quieted. As much as Thomas was an arsehole, his words hurt. Sarah had been in constant jeopardy since Howard had brought her in. As partners went, he was a shitty one.

But what could I have done? Sarah is a lioness. She hunts alone. Without her, the MCU might not have done half the good it has.

"I assembled you all here for an update," said Palu, nodding at some of the senior analysts standing at the back of the room. They weren't often invited to senior meetings. "What do we have? Mandy?"

Mandy flinched as if surprised to be called on. He cleared his throat twice before he summoned words. "The Tower Bridge bombers were spotted arriving in a Toyota Space Cruiser, a relic from the 90s. Not many about—a collector's item, really." He cleared his throat again. "Anyway, I set up a team to trace its history and recent locations."

Palu sneered. "So, you have nothing? Thomas, what about you?"

"I've been working with my contacts in the Middle-East, and they all agree that Shab Bekhier has been dormant for at least the last three years—not including Hesbani's splinter group. My current assumption is that a new group has assembled and taken the name."

"So you don't believe Al-Sharir is behind this?" asked Palu.

"How could he be? The man is wanted by every authority in Europe. If he were still alive, we would have flagged him by now. If a nuclear bomb were in play, it's more likely that this is an Iranian plot—or maybe Pakistani."

Howard shook his head. "Sarah used to be your wife, Tom, and yet you dismiss what she said? She said it was Al-Sharir."

"I am still her husband, Hopkins, but that is beside the point. Sarah has been under a lot of strain, and the topic of Shab Bekhier has rattled her. We're unable to validate what she told us right now. She may already have been stabbed by that point. Blood loss... panic... she's not a reliable witness. I don't want to get sidetracked by looking for phantoms. Our main concern is a potential bomb—nuclear or otherwise—so I suggest you focus on something other than Sarah, Hopkins. Your attachment to her is concerning."

"Excuse me?" said Howard, shifting in his seat. His hands were sweating.

Thomas didn't flinch. "You know exactly what I'm saying. Sarah is not interested in being close to you, Howard, so back off. She's been through enough."

Howard leapt up from his seat. "Because of you, you jackass! Her head has been all over the place since you came out of the desert like the second coming. She thought you were dead. You were dead to her. Notice how she's not been all that keen on talking to you?"

"She just needs some time."

"Don't assume you understand what she needs, Tom. You don't know her."

"She is my wife."

Howard shook his head. "This is her family."

Thomas turned to Palu. "Is this not evidence that Hopkins is unfit to do this job? He sounds more like a love-sick schoolboy than an international agent."

Howard clambered across the table, knowing he was losing control but unable to change course. He grabbed Thomas by the collar. "I'm her partner, you arsehole."

Thomas threw a punch and knocked Howard back across the table. He tumbled awkwardly and sprawled onto some chairs. The analysts at the back of the room gasped. Thomas punched Howard in the ribs while he tried to get back to his feet.

Mandy appeared from nowhere and grabbed Thomas by the arm, swinging him into the nearest wall. Then he dragged Howard to his feet and shoved him away. "You okay?"

Howard rubbed his jaw. "I'll live."

"Suspend him, Palu." Thomas was bright red.

Palu said nothing for a moment, just laced his fingers together and stared at the table. He seemed burdened by more than just the ongoing situation. "If I'm going to suspend anybody," he said, "it will be you, Agent Gellar. Your obvious personal issues with Sarah are causing problems for us all. Agent Hopkins' relationship with Agent Stone has been nothing but professional. Your own jealousy and paranoia is affecting your work. I suggest you take responsibility for the decisions you made five years ago, and stop acting out at other people. You are new to this team, and are very welcome, but if you continue to goad my Agents, or give me orders, I will put you on the first plane back to Disneyland."

Thomas glared at Palu. "If you're referring to my home state of Florida, at least get your facts straight. Disneyland is in California. I think you mean Disney World."

"Wherever the Muppets fuck is of no concern to me, Agent Gellar. What concerns me is the fate of this nation, and right now, you all seem more interested in melodrama. If anyone could see us, we would all be fired on the spot. We have a vital duty. To this country. To each other."

Howard was panting, anger pumping his lungs like a set of bellows. He took a second to calm down, but eventually nodded. "I'm sorry, Gellar. The bad guys scored a victory yesterday, and what happened to Sarah is a little too close to home for us all. I wish I had something that could help us, but the truth is I have nothing. These terrorists appeared out of nowhere and blew up a landmark, taking a local MP and one hundred and nineteen people with them. The MCU exists to keep the gates of hell closed, but today we allowed one of the locks to fall. If we don't act now, the whole thing will blow open."

Thomas stared at his feet and seemed ashamed at his behaviour—maybe he wasn't a complete arsehole. "I just want to help," he said. "I apologise for doing anything other."

"Then let's figure this out," said Palu, "so that the next lunatic with a bomb looks elsewhere to make their statement. We will not allow the United Kingdom to become a soapbox for monsters."

The door to the conference room opened, making them all turn. Dr Bennet frowned at the fallen chairs and the fact that everyone was out of breath. "You know, everyone can hear you kids bickering in here. Y'all might want to keep it down. Our patient is awake, but she has quite the headache."

Howard felt a spark up his back. "Sarah's awake?"

Jessica smiled. "That's what I said now. Want me to see if the lady's taking visitors?"

Everyone in the room smiled, and the tension fell away just a little. It was the good news they needed.

Sarah was awake.

***

Howard entered the quiet space of the infirmary and strode toward a curtained cubicle at the back. Thomas tried to throw out a hand to hold him back, but he missed, so Howard arrived first. He threw back the curtain and smiled to see Sarah awake. "I swear you spend more time in this hospital bed than you do your own."

Sarah managed a weak smile. "That fact you even think about me in bed is weird."

Howard sat on the foot of the bed. "How are you feeling?"

"Like I was stabbed."

Thomas stepped inside. "It's not funny, Sarah. You shouldn't have been in that situation."

She blinked, and for a moment it seemed her eyes might stay closed, but then they drew open slowly. "Situations like what? Trying to stop terrorists and psychopaths? I'm pretty sure that's the exact situation MCU agents are supposed to get into."

"You should have been more careful," he chided. "You could have died."

"Don't worry about it, Tom. Even if I had died, I could just come back from the dead like you."

Thomas exhaled. "Sarah…"

"Thomas."

Howard patted her leg—warm beneath the covers. He didn't want her getting stressed out with the whole Thomas issue. "We're just glad you're okay, Sarah. Jessica said everything will heal fine."

"Except my face," said Sarah, "but hey, look on the bright side—which is on my right, in case you were wondering."

"Glad to see your sense of humour has returned," said Palu, standing by the curtain with Mandy. "I'm sorry to jump straight on your neck, but we need to be clear about what you said on the phone before…"

She nodded. "Before Plant Face stuck a knife in me like a prized pumpkin? I remember: I said Al-Sharir is alive and that he has a nuclear bomb. I wasn't kidding."

The room went silent.

"You're sure?" asked Thomas.

"Al-Sharir was wearing a name badge. And the bomb said nuclear warhead on the side."

Thomas glanced at Howard, unsure how to take Sarah's

sarcasm. Some husband, if he didn't know her sense of humour by now. It led Howard to consider what she must have been like before he'd met her. Before she lost half her face.

And an unborn child.

Howard glared at Thomas. And a husband. That makes three shitty cards life dealt her.

"Look," said Sarah, blinking as if her eyes were irritated. "It was Al-Sharir for sure. He's had a shave, and wears a suit, but I've been seeing that man's face in my dreams every night for the last five years—and not in a good, sexy way. It was him. I'm certain. As for the nuclear bomb, I don't know for sure, because I'm not an atomic brain cheese, but I saw a cylinder inside an open suitcase with Russian writing on it. I'm leaning towards it being very bad."

Thomas sighed as if relieved. "It could be a chemical bomb."

Sarah nodded. "Yeah, let's hope so. That would be lovely."

"Sarah..."

"Thomas."

"So we have a serious problem on our hands," said Palu, rubbing his face with both hands. Despite his Indian heritage, he'd grown deathly pale. "Al-Sharir must have some serious resources to disappear off the radar for so long. No reason he would be in the United Kingdom other than to launch an attack."

Sarah added, "He blames us for every single death in Afghanistan, including his wife, children, and several cousins."

"Then he shouldn't have been a member of the Taliban," said Thomas.

"There's no proof he was," said Sarah. "Al-Sharir is a monster we made."

Howard groaned. "And now he's here."

Sarah looked at Palu. "So, do you believe me?"

Palu took a moment to answer. "Sarah, you are one of the bravest, most intelligent people I've ever known. You are fearless—reckless even—and sometimes you let your heart lead your decisions instead of your head. But I trust you completely. If you say Al-Sharir is here, then he is here. Relax, Sarah. We'll take care of things until you're better."

Howard patted her on the leg again. She looked beaten in a way he hadn't seen before. Eyes dull and lifeless. "I'm sorry you got hurt. I should have been there."

"No kidding," said Thomas.

Sarah gazed at Howard with bleary eyes. "It's my fault. I ran off half-cocked like I always do. If it had been you, you would have called for backup. I'm to blame, no one else."

"Well, you're safe now," said Thomas. "Get better and we'll figure out the rest later. I don't know what I would have done if you..."

Sarah grimaced. "Don't Thomas. Please don't. There's a terrorist and a serial killer loose because of me. Things haven't even started getting bad yet. I'd be better off dead."

"Do you remember anything that can help us, Sarah?" asked Palu eagerly. He was the only one with his mind on business. Howard did not blame him for that. There were bigger issues than Sarah's injury.

Sarah shook her head. "I don't remember what happened after the phone booth. Al-Sharir has set up in an abandoned warehouse somewhere. Opposite an old garage, I think. Sherwood Street? The bomb is in a white van—I didn't get the plates. Maybe a Citroen. I... I'm sorry; my mind's a blur."

"We blanketed the area," said Palu. "We found an empty warehouse, but there was nothing there."

"Mandy found you after we traced your call," explained Howard. "We got to you as fast as we could."

At the back, Mandy nodded solemnly. "I thought you were already gone. But when I picked you up to carry you back to the car, you woke up."

Sarah frowned as if trying to recall. "I don't remember."

"You were delirious from blood loss. It was all over the floor of the phone booth. I can't believe no one saw you. You kept saying something over and over. A name: Katie."

Sarah said nothing, just stared for a moment, then lurched to the side and retched. Howard lunged to keep her from falling out of bed. Jessica came running into the room. She held a cardboard bedpan and shoved it under Sarah's chin.

"Okay, sweetheart. Get it all up. It's just the body coping with shock. Once it's out, it's out."

Sarah stopped vomiting and spat thick wads into the pan for several moments. She let out a painful moan and flopped back into the bed. Howard tried to grab her hand, but she moved it away.

"It's all finished now, Sarah," said Thomas. "You're safe. You don't need to risk your life anymore, you're done. Everything will be okay."

"Let's give her a little peace now, please, boys," said Jessica. "She needs to rest."

Howard stood. Although Sarah's wounds were not life-threatening, she looked like she was scrabbling at death's door. It wasn't only physical—she looked emotionally weak. It hurt Howard to see her. Sarah was so strong, so... stubborn. Seeing her beaten and wounded was not how he wanted to remember her.

And he was feeling like these might be his final moments with her. Sarah wanted out. Looking at her now, it was obvious.

"I'm here if you need me, Sarah," he told her. Then left her alone.

* * *

Sarah stared at the ceiling, willing the sickness away. It didn't matter how tough you were when you vomited; it reduced everyone to a pleading child. Nausea was the least of her worries though. Lying in bed, alone, was not what she needed.

How many people would die because of her?

How many more victims would the Flower Man claim?

When would Al-Sharir's next attack be? And where?

She was an MCU agent—a guardian—and she had failed to do her job. Worst of all, she was quitting that job. The death toll would be on her, and she wasn't even going to stick around to take responsibility.

I can't stay. I have nothing left to give.

I've been beaten, shot at, stabbed.

And how many people have I watched die? Bradley. Ollie. My father.

I've done more than should ever be expected of a person. I never asked for any of it.

"Your body will be just fine, but I'm afraid I can't prescribe anything to remove that dark cloud hanging over your head."

Sarah saw Dr Bennet standing at the foot of her bed and frowned. "Sorry?"

Jessica took a perch by Sarah's legs, scooping her long white coat beneath her. "You're finished, aren't you, sweetheart?"

Sarah nodded, and the act of admission nearly brought tears.

"That's okay. You wouldn't be human if you could let the last year's events slide off your back. I've watched you do things no one else could ever do. I mean, y'all leapt out of a helicopter in mid-air."

The absurdity of the memory made Sarah smile. The thought she had done something so reckless...

It worked though. I jumped out of a helicopter and lived.

"You'll all be better off without my crazy stunts."

Jessica huffed. "If it weren't for your crazy stunts, the Earthworm would have been filled in with concrete months ago. Instead, it's chock full of analysts all working against evil. You did that, Sarah."

"No."

"God made you to be what you are," said Jessica, "and you should never apologise for it. I judged you harshly when you arrived, but now I would be heartbroken to see you leave."

Sarah fought back tears again. "A year ago, I would never have believed you if you'd said I'd have people caring about me."

Jessica smiled.

"It's not enough though. I'm scared—so scared that I feel like my heart might explode in my chest. I don't sleep. I can't eat. Around every corner I expect to see a gun…" She nodded at her mid-section, bandaged and covered by the blanket, "or a knife."

Jessica sighed, reached out and took Sarah's hand. "Sweetheart, let me tell you a story about what it's like to be a frightened woman. Y'all have to go right back to nineteen eighty-eight for a start. Medical College of Georgia. That was where I got my degree. A fine place for doctoring, my daddy called it. I hated it. My family was poor, and I was living off the money I made working at a fried chicken shack. I shared a house with four other girls and got on with none of them—you've probably noticed I take a while to warm up to people."

Sarah nodded. "I like to describe you as socially cautious."

"Then you would be most kind. Anyway, being poor wasn't the reason I hated school. I was homesick."

"Understandable."

"Not at all," said Jessica. "I should have been glad to escape. It should have been the biggest relief in the world."

Sarah frowned. "Why?"

"Because I was away from him."

"Who?"

"Uncle Ted. My daddy's brother."

Sarah swallowed. "I'm not sure I like where this is going."

"You shouldn't, sweetheart, because it's precisely what you think. Back home, I was always my daddy's little angel, but Uncle Ted saw me as something different. To him, I was his dirty little niece he could use however, and whenever, he liked."

Sarah's nausea came back like a tidal wave crashing through her guts.

"It started when I was six or seven," Jessica continued. "Living so close, Uncle Ted would often babysit for my folks. I won't go into detail, but when I grew old enough to leave for school, I thought the abuse was behind me. But I missed home. Ain't that the most insane thing you ever heard?"

Sarah said nothing, not sure she understood enough to respond.

Sensing her confusion, Jessica patted her on the leg beneath the covers. "I missed my daddy and my ma. I missed the tyre swing hanging from the maple in our yard and the smell of the country. Worst of all, I missed him."

"Your uncle?"

"Don't ask me why, but I missed him like the rest of my folks. I think I missed my small, easy to understand world. School was like being in the jungle. People everywhere competing for grades, jobs, friends, social standing. Boys were sniffing around me every time I went for a drink, and they all seemed to have an agenda. Girls were bitchy—just like I feared they'd be. Essays were hard and ever present, and my job selling chicken at two in the morning to drunks and deadbeats was soul crushing. I was drowning, and I missed home where things made sense."

"But you stayed," said Sarah. "You were strong enough to see it through."

She nodded. "Yes, I stayed and finished my education. Turns out, though, home followed me to college. Uncle Tom took a job in Augusta, a mile away. Turned up one day right on campus to see me. I thought I was hallucinating."

Sarah shook her head. "You're kidding me?"

"Nope. He had ideas in his mind of us being together. I was a woman now, and away from home. No one would know. He had a place—small, but much nicer than the single room I had in a house with girls I hated."

"I hope you told him to piss off!"

Jessica didn't answer and looked away.

"Oh..."

Jessica turned her gaze back at Sarah. They were not weeping, but steely and hard. "I let that monster pervert me. As a child, I had no choice, but as a woman, I could have said no. But I was weak and scared, so I clung to him because he was familiar. Whatever I do, Sarah, for as long as I live, I will always be that weak, incestuous girl who moved in with her abusive uncle just to feel safe. If a heart attack hadn't taken him two years later, I'm not sure how it would have ended. I barely talk to my folks anymore; can hardly face them. Shame is a wretched thing, Sarah. No need to tell you that."

Sarah felt tears on her cheeks, unable to hold them back. "That's horrible, Jessica."

She shrugged. "And yet it's nothing."

"What? What do you mean?"

"It's just a single story in this horrible world we inhabit. Men and women make monsters of themselves every day, and countless victims are used and spat out. If I had been a stronger woman like you, Sarah, perhaps I wouldn't have been a victim. Maybe, if someone brave and courageous like you had been around to protect me, I wouldn't be the cold, mistrustful bitch I am today."

"I'm not courageous, Jessica. And you aren't a bitch."

"Yes I am, and yes you are! Sarah, you are the antithesis of men like Al-Sharir and my uncle. You are part of the other side—the side that protects victims before they get preyed on. You're scared, Sarah, but unlike other people, that doesn't stop you. Don't leave. Stay and stop the monsters. You do that, and I promise it will get easier. You will heal."

Sarah closed her eyes and more tears spilled down her cheeks. "How do you know that?"

"Because I have healed," she said. "Trust me, being here, doing this... it's the best way to stop being afraid. We have to be stronger than they are, Sarah. It's harder for us because there's more at stake."

"I don't know if I can keep going."

Jessica stood up from the bed. "You don't know you can't, either. Get some rest. I'll check on you again after Breslow leaves."

Sarah wiped her eyes and tried to sit up. Her stomach wound creased and pain flared. "The Prime Minister is here?"

"Not yet, but she's on her way. Nobody knows what she wants, but all senior team members are ordered to attend. You're probably lucky to get to sit this one out. It's unlikely she'll be happy."

"Yeah," said Sarah. "Lucky."

Heads will roll, and it's all my fault.

* * *

Jessica left Sarah alone, but she found herself incapable of sleep. Painkillers helped with the pain, but it was persistent enough to keep her from comfort. Her wound, stitched and bandaged, felt hot beneath the covers. Despite her injuries, Sarah's mind was on other things.

Why is Breslow coming here?

Does she blame the MCU for Tower Bridge?

Of course she does. Who else is to blame?

I am to blame. As much as everyone else, I am to blame.

Palu would try to take the blame personally, Sarah knew, but Howard would jump in and share it with him. Jessica would probably stay silent—Mandy for sure. Thomas would...

Sarah had no idea how Thomas would react, and that upset her. Did she even know him anymore? It had been five years.

There had been a time when Sarah thought she knew Thomas better than anyone. A time when she had loved everything about the man. Was he that same, caring person she'd planned to move to Florida with? The man she was going to settle down and live the quiet life with?

How did life get so complicated?

Sarah gritted her teeth and pushed herself into a sitting position. It hurt like hell—took her breath away—but it didn't floor her. She was able to catch her breath. Once she was sure her stitches had not reopened, she rotated her hips and tossed her legs over the side of the bed, sliding forward until her bare feet touched the frigid tiles.

God damn, her stomach hurt.

She stood up slowly, breathing heavily. An invisible hand socked her in the stomach, but she attempted to walk it off. One foot in front of the other, she took a step.

Okay, okay. This isn't so bad.

Sarah shuffled across the infirmary. She wore a hospital gown, but located her boots and stepped into them. Getting into her clothes, though, would be too much, so she headed for the door.

The infirmary lay in the Earthworm's middle section. The middle section also housed the Hive, which was where a majority of the MCU's analysts worked in a giant open workspace. That was where Sarah came out on her way to the head-section. Two hundred analysts stopped what they were doing and stared. A hospital gown was not the most professional dress for a senior field agent.

Sarah cleared her throat. "I want a team working on the location of my clothes, stat. I want last known locations, possible associates, the works."

The analysts continued to stare.

Sarah bellowed at them. "All right, get back to work!"

Shit that hurt. Okay, then, no more shouting.

Two colleagues came to help Sarah, but she waved them away. She limped on her own through the Hive and tried not to collapse where anybody would see. The head section of the Earthworm lay ahead, and it was where Breslow would be if she was already in the building.

She took fifteen minutes to get there, by which time she was too weak to push open the heavy door to the conference room. Through the frosted glass silhouettes moved. Words were exchanged.

Sarah knocked on the glass.

The door opened.

Howard's wide eyes peered out at her. "Sarah?"

"I wanted to check if anyone fancied a cuppa."

Jessica pushed Howard aside and appeared in the doorway. "Sarah, what are you doing out of bed? Actually, how are you out of bed? I gave you enough painkillers to dope a horse."

"Good thing I'm not a horse then. Is Breslow here?"

Jessica nodded her head to the side subtly. "Yes, she's inside."

"I need to be in on this. I'm responsible."

"Sarah, no-"

"Bloody well let her in," came a stern voice. "Stop wasting time."

Jessica sighed and moved aside so that Sarah could step inside the conference room. Sure enough, Prime Minister Breslow stood there with her hands on her hips. The stocky, short-haired brunette was pushing sixty, but she glared as fiercely as any woman in her prime.

Sarah nodded. "Prime Minister."

"Agent Stone. I wish I could say it was nice to see you, or that you're looking well, but alas I seem to run into you at the worst times."

Sarah couldn't think of anything to say, so she went over to the room's large oval table. Thomas pulled a chair out for her, but when he tried to help her sit, she shoved him away and lowered herself into the seat. She wished the back support weren't so rigid.

"Okay," said Breslow. "Can we get back to it, please? I was just in the middle of promising to close down the MCU and drag you all through the muck. Again, I state that Tower Bridge is currently sinking into the Thames. A hundred-and-twenty-two-year-old landmark gone forever because someone here wasn't doing their job." She slammed her fists on the table. "Somebody better have a damn good reason why this was allowed to happen."

Palu placed both his own hands on the desk as if to brace himself. "It's my fault," he said shakily. "The MCU had no knowledge of this attack. That is down to me as leader of this team."

"No," said Howard. "We all work together and if something was missed, we all missed it."

"Then you're all murderers," said Breslow. "One hundred and sixteen deaths are on you. Your job is to stop terrorists, and damn did you ever screw the fucking pooch this time."

"Again, I take full responsibility," said Palu.

"It's clear, mistakes have been made," Thomas interjected. "I intend to investigate fully what went wrong, Prime Minister."

On who's authority, thought Sarah. Palu is the boss, not you.

"Not now you won't," Breslow told Thomas. "I'm not here to find out who needs lynching. There'll be time for that later. There's going to be another attack, and you have less than twelve hours to stop it."

"How do you know?" asked Sarah. It was precisely as she'd feared; more deaths would be on her hands. If she hadn't turned her back on the Flower Man in that phone booth, she could have brought in a team to take out Al-Sharir before he escaped.

Breslow nodded to an aide who Sarah hadn't even noticed was standing in the room. The man had an obvious talent for fading into the background. Now, he slunk forward and placed a small laptop onto the table. He used a cable to plug it into the media port built into the conference table. The laptop's display came up on the room's 65inch wall monitor.

"The media aren't running this yet—on my orders—but I can only keep it from the public for so long. It took place this morning in front of a police station in Croydon."

Sarah watched the monitor with trepidation. Yet again, she witnessed a video of a London street. This time, the focus was on one man. Light-skinned, yet potentially Middle-Eastern, he wore perhan tunban—the traditional dress of an Afghani man. He looked directly at the camera as he spoke, spitting every word with venom.

"Prime Minister Breslow, for a decade you have waged war on Allah's true people. You have reduced our homes to rubble. You have taken our possessions and raped our land. Money is your idol. Greed your weapon. Today, you reap what you have sown.

Already your golden city burns, but your empire has only just begun to crumble. Within twenty-four hours, we will decimate your heathen empire. We will inflict upon your golden city a death toll from which it will never recover." The man paused for a moment as if wanting his words to sink in. "The only way to prevent this is repentance. Prime Minister Breslow, accept that your life is beyond saving and end it. You have twelve hours in which to hang yourself to death on national television. Refuse and your empire will burn. One death in exchange for thousands. A true leader loves his people. Are you a true leader?"

Sarah expected the video to end, but instead, the man threw up his loose-fitting shirt and exposed several sticks of explosives wrapped around his bare stomach. Two seconds later, the man's body was replaced by a cloud of billowing smoke. A single sandal remained on the ground.

The video ended. Breslow stepped in front of the television. "As if my day couldn't get any bloody worse. The deadline is 8PM tonight. I'm not intending to hang myself, so I suggest you put a stop to these maniacs before they carry out their next attack. Fail and I will hang you out to dry like you wouldn't believe. You'll go down in history as the most inept group of people who ever lived. I will not condone any more of my public being murdered. Enough is enough. Get your shit together, folks. Palu, I want a word with you in private."

Palu nodded and followed the Prime Minister out of the room like a scalded dog. The PM's aid disappeared with them.

A long moment of silence filled the room while those remaining stared at one another blankly.

Sarah broke the tension, "Has anyone told Breslow about the nuclear bomb yet?"

Chapter 6

Three hours and nothing. The MCU's senior team—the country's foremost counter-intelligence personnel—were without leads of any kind. The minutes ticked by, and soon those minutes would make up hours. Hours they didn't have. Mandy sat in silence typing away, while Jessica anxiously hummed. Howard and Palu conversed over a shared monitor while Thomas glanced periodically at Sarah. Sarah acted as though she didn't notice.

Jessica had given her a pain injection which allowed her to function, and luckily it did little to dull her mind. Unluckily, however, it did nothing to dull her emotions. Her hands trembled.

Palu had returned ten minutes after leaving to talk with Breslow, more rattled than ever. He shared nothing with the rest of them, but he'd clearly been held accountable. A sheen of sweat coated his forehead, and he cleared his throat constantly as he worked. Unlike the conference room, the war room featured no central table, and instead, featured a circular bank of slimline computers. Any agent could bring up a document on screen and zip it across to another terminal. It allowed the senior agents to work fast and as a team. Howard was zipping something across multiple screens right now.

"I have a background on the bomber in front of the police station," he explained. "Nasir Riaz, twenty-four years old. Comes from a good family. Father's a solicitor. Mother's an estate agent. No siblings. He is a confirmed Muslim, but has no ties to extremist groups or foreign interests. I'm waiting on a search of his internet history, but so far there's nothing about him that cries terrorist. Wait, hold on a second..."

"What is it?" Sarah asked. She sat directly to his left.

Howard frowned at the screen for two seconds before speaking. "I have Riaz's education in front of me. He completed a Modern Language degree at University of Exeter and has been studying a Master's degree at University College London... in Russian Studies."

Thomas shrugged. "Russian, so?"

"It could be something," suggested Howard.

Thomas pulled a face. "Not Russia's style. Think again, Hopkins."

"No, wait," said Sarah, putting up a hand. "Back at the warehouse, right after I escaped, there was a guard. He was speaking into a phone. I swear he was speaking Russian. And the other men—Al-Sharir's men—were not all Middle-Eastern. Some of them were white. They could have been Russians."

Palu knitted his hands together and closed his eyes as if he had a headache. "Okay, okay, that may be something we can use, but... I don't know. Something feels off. Islam and Moscow don't tend to see eye to eye. The Russians shed as much blood in Afghanistan as we did. I can't see Al-Sharir working with them."

"Al-Sharir always thinks about the big picture," said Sarah. "I'm not saying these attacks came from Putin himself, but there's plenty of wealthy factions within Russia that would benefit from a destabilised West. Al-Sharir would have needed money and influence to disappear for years while he planned this. He hasn't been seen in the Middle East at all. Maybe that's because he was in Russia or Eastern Europe."

"Okay. We run with it," said Palu. "Howard, get me a list of all the students taking Russian Studies at UCL. See if you can contact Riaz's tutor. The more we can learn about the kid, the better."

"I'll check flights out of Russia during the last month," said Jessica. "Maybe Al-Sharir came in under an alias."

"Okay," said Palu, "but don't linger on that because it might be a dead end. Palm it off to an analyst quick as you can."

"Should we send a team out into the field?" asked Howard. "We need eyes on the streets."

"I've already sent out everything we have to surveil every London landmark we can think of. I even recalled Mattock from his new recruits."

Sarah relaxed at hearing Mattock was returning. The bolshy Mancunian was as tough as they came, and a calming influence in even the worst of shit storms. He had been off training new field agents in the Brecon Beacons using techniques he'd learned in the SAS. They needed him back now more than ever.

"What should I focus on?" asked Sarah, hating that she needed direction. Her mind was a blur.

"You should go back to the infirmary," said Thomas. "Sarah, we got this. I don't want you injuring yourself further."

"I'm fine."

"You're tough," he admitted, "but you're not invincible. You were stabbed one day ago. Most normal people would be in agony."

"I am in agony," she said. "But this is my mess. I need to clean it up."

"This isn't your mess, Sarah." Howard sighed. "Al-Sharir got by us all."

"But the Flower Man didn't. I had him. And if I hadn't dropped my guard, I would still have him and would have called a team in quickly enough to stop Al-Sharir. I screwed up. So shut up and let me unscrew things. We have..." she checked her watch, "six hours until we all potentially explode. I just need a place to start."

The intercom in the centre of the room buzzed.

Palu reached forward and pulled one of the handsets from its cradle. He spoke into the receiver. "What is it? Okay... What? Have you verified?" He took the handset away from his ear and glanced across the table, at Sarah.

She frowned. "What is it?"

"We have a phone call. It's the Flower Man."

Sarah reached out and yanked one of the intercom handsets and placed it to her ear. The pain in her stomach seemed far away. "Hello."

"Meadow? Is that you, Meadow?"

"Yes, it's Sarah."

"Impressive. You don't die easy. Strong roots."

"Maybe if you weren't such an idiot, you would have stabbed me properly."

Thomas's jaw dropped, and he reached out for the intercom. Sarah smacked him away. On the other end of the line, the Flower Man chuckled. "You and I have had a taxing experience. You're not the only one licking your wounds. Nature heals though, and so will we."

"What do you want? I know it's not to tell us where you are. Have you been thinking about me? Sorry to hurt your big serial-killer ego, but I'm focused on other things right now, so could you leave a message with my secretary, please?"

"Oh, Meadow, I will enjoy what remains of our time together, but I am not calling because I miss you, my sweet pea. That you're even alive is news to me. No, I am calling about our little problem back there in the warehouse."

"The bomb?"

"Yes, that vile, manmade abomination. You must stop it. London is my home."

"How touching."

"I dislike terrorists as much as you do. So messy and meaningless. I can help you, Meadow."

Sarah looked up and realised all eyes were on her. The call was now on speaker, and an analyst would be running a trace. "Sorry, we're not hiring."

"I know what your friend is planning next."

Sarah gripped the handset tighter. "How could you know that?"

"Because I speak Russian—like that guard did before you knocked him out."

Sarah remembered the Flower Man squinting back at the warehouse as if thinking. No, he was listening. "You understood what he was saying."

"Yes. People are going to die, Meadow. Lots of people."

"Tell me what you heard."

"No. I was going to, but now that I know you're alive..."

"What do you want?"

"A meeting."

"Where?"

He told her, and Sarah didn't waste a second agreeing to the time and place.

"But Sarah, I expect you to come alone. If I see anybody else, I will hold onto this information until the next life. If we're going to work together, I expect you to keep your word."

"It will be me alone, you have my word. But if you try anything, or if this is some bullshit ploy, then I'll shoot you in the face."

There was a brief pause, then the line went dead.

The call ended, and Sarah replaced the handset.

Palu called for the trace. The call had been made from a payphone in the middle of Harrow. A team was already en route.

"There's no way you are going to that ambush," Thomas said to Sarah. "It's madness."

"You got anything else? Nope, didn't think so."

Howard sighed. "It's dangerous, Sarah."

"This job is dangerous."

"Okay. I'll be close by with backup. I won't be more than two minutes away." Howard said.

Thomas threw his arms up. "What is happening here? Are you all actually considering this?"

"I don't know," said Sarah. "Are we?" She stared straight at Palu, who had been absent from the discussion so far. Something was on his mind, and it was making him indecisive.

Palu nodded slowly, then addressed Thomas directly. "We have nothing else, Gellar. We can't afford to turn down the only Intel we have."

"You'll get her killed."

"No," said Sarah, rising from her chair "I am choosing to do this, so if something happens, it's on me. I don't need you looking after me, so back off, okay?"

Thomas looked at her like she was mad. "Fine. What do I care? I'm only your husband."

With that, Thomas turned and left the war room.

***

Sarah rubbed her shoulders as she stood exposed outside of the garden centre. It wasn't particularly cold, but she couldn't help shivering. A symptom of the blood she had lost. She felt weak too, although better than she had. The more she moved about and walked, the less stiff her body felt. With the injection Jessica had given her before leaving, she might almost pass for uninjured. She just hoped she wouldn't have to run or defend herself. It would not end well.

Arranging a meeting inside a garden centre in Croydon was an attempt at irony or the Flower Man held such delusions that he genuinely needed to be around plants. Did he think he was a plant? No, he wasn't that crazy.

Just the level of crazy that makes you torture and mutilate innocent people.

Am I actually about to do this?

Just pop in for a chat with a serial killer, Sarah. What's the worst that can happen? It's not like you're wounded from his previous attempt to kill you.

Sarah cleared her throat and stepped inside.

Mid-afternoon on a Saturday, which meant the garden centre was crammed with people. The narrow aisles of plants and shrubs made it hard to check out the entire area at first glance. People bunched up in several chokepoints as they tried to manoeuvre trolleys around one another. Standing amongst so many colourful flowers, Sarah would have expected perfume, but she only smelled soil. The air dripped with the moist, earthy odour of it.

No sign of the Flower Man.

Sarah chose the first aisle and walked down it, brushing past a row of overhanging hydrangeas. Their pink and blue petals bunched together like a clown's wig. Their beauty was lost on Sarah. People with scarred faces care little about flowers. It was her scars people looked at now, moving to other aisles to avoid her. People didn't trust themselves not to stare, so they avoided the situation by moving away. Nothing Sarah was unused to. People kept their distance from ugly.

Except Howard and the others.

If I leave the MCU, I'll have nobody.

I was doing just fine before I met Howard.

Were you, Sarah? she asked herself, *because I seem to recall you getting into a fight in the middle of a bank.*

Sarah shook away her thoughts and carried on down the aisle. She had a job to do, and she was distracting herself. The odds of her walking out of that garden centre in one piece were slim, so the least she could do was concentrate.

At the rear of the giant greenhouse was an opening to the outside that appeared to be where all the taller shrubs and potted trees were arranged. It was there that Sarah headed, hoping to find room to manoeuvre. The garden centre's interior was muggy, cramped, and made her claustrophobic.

"Meadow."

Sarah turned and saw a figure emerge from the mingling branches of a row of ferns. The Flower Man. His face was yellowed and knotted from his beatings, but he had recovered well—better than she had. He stood straight, long limbs poised. His eyes smouldered fiercely.

"I was beginning to think you wouldn't come," said Sarah coyly. She hoped to disguise her frailty by goading him.

"I always keep my word, Meadow, as you apparently keep yours. I saw no one else arrive."

Sarah, looking around at the shrubs and potted trees. "I have to ask: What is the deal with the whole gardener thing? Did your mother sleep with a daffodil or something?"

His expression darkened.

Sarah noted the reaction and prodded a little more. "Is your mother still alive? Does she know what you do?"

"My mother is of no concern to you, but she would be proud of what I have become."

Sarah noted the words would have and become. What did he feel he had become? No time to psychoanalyse a killer right now though. "Okay, we can get into it another time, I suppose. Once you're locked up."

The Flower Man smirked. "You came alone as promised, but you don't hide your pain as well as you think. A strong breeze could knock you over."

"It's only a matter of time until we catch you. You've been exposed."

"And like a rose bush exposed to the sun, I will flourish. That is why I must insist you stop your friend."

Sarah snarled. "He's not my friend."

"He seemed to think otherwise. Regardless, he's just another one of you: a destroyer out to reduce the world to rubble. You will stop him. My work is not yet done."

"What is Al-Sharir planning? You said you knew."

"I know the next target will kill ninety thousand."

Sarah wobbled as she heard that terrifying number. Ninety thousand! A spike of pain burst through her wounded abdomen and almost floored her. To her surprise, the Flower Man reached out and steadied her.

"Not yet, Meadow. Stay focused."

"You're sure—ninety thousand?"

"Yes, I am positive. It must be the bomb we saw."

"Where will it go off?"

The Flower Man frowned, recalling. "I don't know. The guard said something about it being ironic that this country was going to be brought to its knees by one of the false idols it worships."

"What the hell does that mean?"

"Your job to work it out, Meadow, not mine. I've told you what I know."

"Which is nothing!"

"I have faith in you. If you succeed, we will meet again. Perhaps just the once more. I tire easily."

Sarah reached out. "Wait! You're not going anywhere."

He yanked on her arm and kicked her knee, tripping her to the ground. The impact of her ribs hitting the gravelled floor knocked the air from her lungs and sent a shock wave of agony through her wounded torso. She yelled out, but her attacker clamped a hand over her mouth. "You disappoint me, Meadow. You keep trying to end our relationship prematurely. I want to play. You think I missed all your vital organs on accident back in that phone booth? I wanted merely to escape, not end our fun."

The Flower Man fumbled with her belt. Startled spectators called for help, but no one intervened to help her.

"Get off me," Sarah moaned.

The Flower Man pulled her radio free and tossed it into the row of ferns. "And no calling your friends on me. We'll meet again—don't you worry."

Before turning away, the Flower Man booted Sarah in the stomach, making her shriek. Then he was gone, disappearing into the potted ferns.

* * *

Her wedding night. Damn, she could hardly believe it. A year in one of the harshest places on earth, and she had found the man of her dreams and married him. It would be difficult, flitting back and forth between camps and trying to plan their down time together, but the ceremony today in front of the Camp Bastian chaplain had been perfect. Too bad her dad hadn't been there to see it. He was currently in whereabouts unknown with the SAS. He had spent half of her life as a ghost. Marrying a military officer might actually have been the thing to gain his approval. The thought of her settling down and being a 'woman' would likely please him. She'd never seen him less happy than when she had tried to gain entry to the SAS to be closer to him. The suspicious part of her wondered if he had been the masked instructor who had put her through the worst hell of her life. She'd almost died going through the assessments, and towards the end, she had become sure she was being put through more than was necessary.

But tonight was not about the past. It was about her future. Her future as both a wife and Army officer. She was a woman and a soldier—and proud to be both. She was living the equality that she sought so desperately to give to the women of Afghanistan. The Taliban would fall, and they would finally get the chance to live their lives.

"You're deep in thought," said Thomas, lying on the bed, naked and sweaty beside her. He ran his finger lightly down her cheek as he looked into her eyes. "Are you really my beautiful wife?"

"Apparently," she said. "Any buyer's remorse?"

He shook his head like she was ridiculous. "Never! Marrying you was my purpose in life."

She rubbed her foot against his ankle. "Don't be silly."

"I'm not. I'm going to love you forever."

"Really?" Something about the thought of having someone care about her—truly care about her—made her flush with happiness and a feeling of safety and certainty that life would always be okay. She'd always be safe.

Thomas kissed her lips. "I'll always be here, Sarah. I promise."

"Good, because up until now, the men in my life have been pretty absent. I need something I can rely on. You make me feel so strong, so protected. I never thought I would ever feel this way, but I love you so much."

"I love you too." Thomas got up from the bed and walked naked around the small bunk-room they had been given for tonight. Sarah's squad had decorated it with a mixture of roses and condoms. Three bottles of champagne sat unopened on the table; they'd been too occupied to make a start on it yet. Thomas went to the bottles now and opened one. Army champagne was not known for its quality, but Sarah's dry mouth cried out for it. Thomas poured them both a glass and then perched on the bed. The desert was freezing tonight, yet both their bodies gleamed with sweat. Their love-making had been wild and fierce, both of them unable to get enough of the other. Sarah knew such passion could not last forever, that marriage was a system of diminishing returns in the sex department, but right now she felt like a higher being, one made of an energy almost too powerful to contain.

Thomas offered a toast. "To our lives together, and our love that will never fade or break."

Sarah clinked her glass. "And to be there for each other no matter what."

They downed their drinks and threw aside their plastic flutes, suddenly thirsty for something other than champagne—thirsty for each other.

Chapter 7

Howard hurried into the garden centre. Sarah had called from her mob-sat, but explained that the Flower Man had first tossed it to get a head start. She wasted five minutes searching for it. Howard had parked outside a nearby supermarket, but London traffic meant he took four minutes to arrive. By the time he reached Sarah, the Flower Man had a ten-minute head start.

"Mandy is circling the main roads," explained Howard. "And we have two teams coming in any minute."

"We won't get him," said Sarah. "He picked this place, which means he would have had an escape route already planned. The only reason he didn't just spill over the phone was because he wanted to torment me."

His partner winced with pain, and blood spotted the front of her shirt where her stitches split. She sat with a cup of tea in one hand that a member of staff had made for her. She didn't try to stand.

"Are you okay?" he asked her. "Do you need me to call an ambulance?"

She shook her head. "I'm hurt, but I'll live. There was never any chance of me arresting him. That's not why I came."

"I know. Hold on, let me get Palu on the line." He glanced around. The staff had cleared the yard and left them alone, so he made the call and put it on loud speaker. "Palu? I'm with Sarah."

Palu responded. "Go ahead, Sarah."

Sarah leaned forward in her chair and wheezed as she spoke. "The Flower Man heard something back at the warehouse. The next attack will kill ninety thousand."

"Ninety thousand?" said Palu. "That exact number?"

"Yes."

Howard rubbed at his chin. "An odd number to just throw out there."

Sarah nodded. "It sounds exact. Maybe the population of an intended blast radius? We should check neighbourhood statistics."

"Already on it," came Thomas's voice. Sarah grimaced, and Howard empathised with her. Every time she looked at Thomas, or heard his voice, it caused her pain.

Is it because she still loves him?

How can she after five years?

Howard knew nothing about Sarah's marriage—it was long before they met—and part of him was uncomfortable with that. It felt like he had got to know Sarah so well over the last year, but the truth was he knew so little.

Why did that bother him?

"Thank you, Agent Gellar," said Sarah coldly.

"Are you hurt?" he asked her. "What happened?"

"I'm okay. The Flower Man escaped, but I expected it."

"That's okay, Sarah. We're doing big picture right now. We'll sweat the small stuff later."

"Deadline is two hours away," said Palu. "Is that all you have, Sarah, or is there more?"

Howard chewed his bottom lip. Two hours. It already felt too late. Was there really a nuclear bomb? Would he get caught in the blast?

No, don't think like that. There's still time.

"One other thing," said Sarah. "Something about the bomb being delivered by one of the idols we worship."

"The hell does that mean?"

"Same thing I asked. I don't know."

Howard looked up at the sky, hoping for inspiration. Night was falling, and it had grown cold. The sun was still low in the sky, but the moon had already appeared as if eager to get started. Was it only a matter of hours before both would be obscured by a choking-black mushroom cloud? Would it be years before London saw the sun again?

Howard closed his eyes. Is it time to pray?

"I'm sending Mandy to come and get you both," said Palu over the radio. "I want you both mobile in case we get a potential location. Stand by."

Sarah tipped the mug of cold tea onto the ground and watched it splash amongst the pebbles. It seemed a somehow portentous gesture to Howard. She looked up at him and said, "This is really bad, isn't it?"

Howard nodded. "About as bad as things get. I'm sorry."

"What for?"

"For dragging you out of your life a year ago, and into this."

Sarah seemed taken aback. She opened her mouth to say something, but a hissing sound interrupted her. "Sarah," came a voice through her mob-sat. "It's Mandy. I'm outside."

Sarah pushed herself up. "We're on our way."

Howard took her arm to help her walk and was pleased when she let him.

* * *

Howard was worried. Worried because when they met Mandy outside the garden centre, Sarah slumped across the backseat, bleeding.

"We need to get you looked over," said Howard. "Your stitches are torn."

She straightened up and lay her head back against the rest. "I'm fine. I just need a breather. We don't have time to worry about a couple of burst stitches. How long until the deadline?"

"One-hour twenty," said Mandy, tapping the digital clock on the Range Rover's lit-up dashboard. It was pitch-black outside, and as Mandy pulled onto the main road, they passed into and out of street lights.

"I should've never run from that warehouse," said Sarah.

Howard turned around in the front passenger seat. "Enough with that bullshit. You couldn't have done anything else, other than getting yourself killed."

"I was terrified, Howard!" The outburst surprised him, and from the shakiness in her voice alone, he realised Sarah was risking a breakdown. "I was fucking scared," she went on manically. "I just wanted to run. Al-Sharir got away with a nuclear bomb because I'm a goddamn coward. What's wrong with me? I'm losing it."

Howard looked at his partner and wanted to hold her. A year ago, he had found a strong, stubborn warrior of a woman and turned her into a bleeding, weeping mess. If anyone was to blame for anything, it was him. "Sarah, what you've been through this last year... I thought you were disposable. When I recruited you, I thought you were disposable. I wanted your knowledge of Shab Bekhier, but no way did I think you were strong enough to become an MCU agent. On paper, you were a train wreck: post-traumatic stress, agoraphobia, anger-issues—and that was just the stuff your follow-up psych listed from when they discharged you from the Army. I thought you were a liability the second I came across your file, but I needed your knowledge, so I used you."

Sarah didn't blink or respond in any way.

"Truth is, though," Howard continued. "Without you, I wouldn't be half the agent I am. This city would likely be in ruins. If I hadn't recruited you when I did, the monsters would have already won. I became an MCU agent because a monster killed my father, but you, Sarah... you're the reason I stay. You show me what an MCU agent is supposed to be. You're brave—like, superhero brave—and if this whole city goes up in flames an hour from now, the last person I would blame for anything is you. You've already done more than you ever had to. Thank you, Sarah, I mean it. For being willing to jump on a grenade if it means saving a life."

Sarah started to cry, but she kept it silent and turned away, looking out of the window at the passing shops and office blocks. Howard didn't know if his words meant anything to her, but they meant something to him. It felt good telling her how he saw her. Maybe it made him less guilty.

The dashboard comm buzzed and Mandy answered the call with his thumb. "Mandy."

"Mandy, it's Palu. Do you have Sarah and Howard?"

"They're in the car with me. You're on speaker."

"Okay, thanks. Howard, Sarah, we're running simulations on blast radius for a low-yield dirty bomb. It could be anywhere in the city. The estimate is based on far too many variables. There's no way to predict where ninety thousand people would be a likely number of casualties other than it being an area with residential tower blocks or heavy commercial areas like Oxford Street. Only places we can rule out are industrial areas. Please tell me you have something else. I need more data to filter the potential target areas."

"We have nothing," said Howard, a lead weight sliding down his throat and thudding in his lower intestines. His leg shook in the foot well, and he had to place a hand on his thigh to stop it.

"Damn it," came Palu. "This country's blood will be on our hands."

Howard glanced in the rearview mirror and saw Sarah grimace. "Come on, Palu. It's not over yet."

But Palu was gone. Thomas broke the silence by coming on the line. "Sarah? Sarah, are you there?"

Howard glanced back at her. As always, she was pained by her husband's presence. Yet, this time, it seemed to revive her as she sat straighter and became more alert. "I'm here."

"Sarah, get out of the city."

"What?"

"There's nothing you can do. You have an hour left, so get your ass back to the Earthworm, or drive even further."

"I can't," she said, shaking her head and seeming to shed some of her weakness. "You expect me to flee when millions of people don't even know they're in danger? How could I live with myself if I ran now? My job is to protect people, and that means sticking around," she looked at Howard, "and jumping on a grenade if I have to."

"What? Sarah, don't be foolish. I know you want to do the right thing, but so do I. We had something real—our marriage—and I shattered it. I shattered it because I wanted to do the right thing. Thousands of people are alive today because of the intelligence I provided. The sacrifice I made, I couldn't say no to—you wouldn't have either, Sarah. Now I want to make things right. We were on our way, Sarah, ready to settle down with a house and kids. Church on Sunday, football on a Monday. You say you're willing to jump on a grenade? Well, that's exactly what

I did five years ago. I jumped on a grenade and destroyed my life because I couldn't stand by and watch innocent people die. Maybe you'll never forgive me, Sarah, but if you die, we'll never get a chance to find out. Loving you was the only thing I had out there in the desert to hold on to. The only thing that was real."

Sarah was frowning, not from confusion, but as if the words hit her hard. Howard had to admit that Thomas sounded genuine, and if it were true, maybe he had done the right thing all along. It took people willing to sacrifice for the rest of the world to be ordinary and selfish. Thomas and Sarah obviously had that in common. Perhaps that was why they'd married. Maybe they would remain so.

"What did you just say?" asked Sarah.

Thomas sounded confused, his voice stuttering for a moment. "What? I don't have time to repeat all that, Sarah, so I really hope you caught it all. I love you. Don't die on me, okay?"

"No, no," she said, seeming to think hard. "What did you say about the house and kids?"

"Erm... Church on Sunday and football on a Monday?"

"Football is on a Saturday," she muttered.

"Not in America, it isn't," replied Thomas. "Sarah...?"

"Shush. It's Saturday today. Is there any football on?"

"You mean soccer?" asked Thomas. "On in the city right now? Why?"

Sarah looked at Howard, but he could only shrug at her. Football wasn't his game. "I only watch Rugby."

Sarah cursed. What was she thinking?

"England are playing Algeria at Wembley," said Mandy. "And it's football, Thomas, because we actually use our feet—not our hands."

Sarah and Howard both turned to Mandy in surprise. "You like football?" Howard asked his long-time colleague. He hadn't known.

Mandy slowed for a traffic light. "Not a lot to do when you spend most your day driving. Football on the radio is one of my few joys—especially when Tottenham are playing."

"And there's football on tonight?" said Sarah. Thomas tried to come back through the line, but she shushed him again. "At Wembley?"

Mandy nodded.

Sarah seemed excited. "Do you know the capacity of Wembley Stadium, Mandy?"

"Ninety thousand."

"Shit! The bomb is at Wembley Stadium."

"How do you know?" asked Thomas through the line.

"Because you don't quote ninety thousand unless you mean ninety thousand. Killed by one of the false idols we worship. People in this country worship footballers. We pay them millions of pounds a year—Al-Sharir said it himself when I was tied up. Footballers are untouchable. And one of them is a terrorist."

Howard was about to turn to Mandy and tell him to change direction for Wembley Stadium, but Mandy was already way ahead of him. He blew the red light, zipping between a black cab and a Tesco delivery van—making both beep irritably—then pulled a one-eighty in the middle of the road. Tyres screeching, they sped off in the opposite direction.

"I think we're on our way to Wembley Stadium," said Howard into the radio. "Maybe you should have the bomb squad meet us there."

"I'm on it," said Palu, back on the line and finally sounding like he had some of his fire back. It was long overdue.

Did they really have a chance?

Howard glanced in the rearview mirror and smiled.

In the back seat, Sarah seemed to be alive again.

***

Sarah still hurt—it felt like she'd stopped a runaway train with her belly button—but the rush of adrenaline had restarted her system. The last thing she wanted was to run headlong into danger, but neither could she run away; something inside of her wouldn't allow it. That was why she'd resigned herself to the nightmare of a bomb crippling London—and perhaps getting caught in its blast. Though she tried not to admit it to herself, death seemed almost certain now.

Perhaps that's why she was doing this.

Death. An end.

There was a chance for her to stop the bomb now though, to prevent more blood being on her hands; a chance to walk away from this with her soul intact. But adrenaline alone wouldn't be enough to keep her going—a virulent spike already fading. Something in her pocket would help her do what needed to get done.

Before leaving the Earthworm, Sarah swiped another painkiller injection from the infirmary's supply closet. The label read: Ketorolac+epinephrine. A combined stimulant and painkiller to help injured agents escape the field before collapsing from their injuries. Right now, Sarah needed it to send her back into the field. She pulled the cap off with her teeth.

Howard caught sight of her in the rearview mirror and spun around. "What the hell is that?"

"A snack," Sarah told him.

Before Howard could object, Sarah speared her thigh with the injector. A tingling wave flooded her body, but a minute later the throbbing agony in her torso subsided. She let out a sigh. Her body relaxed on the backseat.

"I really hope Jessica prescribed you whatever you just shot yourself up with," said Howard.

"That's between me and my doctor. Just stay focused on what matters. Has Palu run a background check on the players?"

"Not yet. He will get back to us as soon as he finds something."

"It better be soon. We have about forty minutes left until London gets the biggest fireworks show in its history."

She knew Howard understood the stakes. Looking out for her was just one of the ways he coped, even though it never failed to irritate her. "You know, there might not be any attack," he suggested. "You escaping the warehouse might have thrown Al-Sharir's plans into disarray."

"I hope not," said Sarah.

"What? Why?"

"Because if I'm right about the stadium, we have a chance to disarm and confiscate that bomb, but if Al-Sharir moves to Plan B, we have nothing. This way is better, even if we're cutting it close."

He looked at the clock on the dashboard. "That's an understatement. You know if the bomb squad can't disarm the device, there's a good chance we'll have front row seats when it goes off."

"Are you saying we should make a run for it while we still can? Let the Bombies handle it?"

"No, I want to see this through. If they can't diffuse the bomb, we can at least report back as much as we can before we're done. We need to be there no matter what, in case there are clues. This is our screw-up."

Thomas came on the line. Mandy turned up the volume. "Bomb squad is outside the stadium. They arrived in an ice cream van."

Howard huffed. "Sorry, what?"

"They turned up in a fake ice cream van to avoid mass panic—apparently, it's something they've been trialling. The vehicle houses a blast container made from Ballistic Fibreglass and coated with flame retardant plastic. If they can't disarm the bomb, they'll remove it to the blast container."

"That's good," said Sarah, "because I was going to throw a blanket over it and hope for the best."

Howard chuckled.

"I've been speaking to stadium security," Thomas went on, "and they are adamant that a bomb could not have made it inside. They almost laughed at the suggestion. Every person through the turnstiles gets searched if they so much as have a purse."

"What about the players?" asked Sarah.

"The players enter through an underground access directly from their coaches. The changing rooms and office facilities are not accessible from the public entrances."

"It came in with one of the players," said Howard. "They wouldn't have been searched."

"Okay?" said Thomas. "But how does a player carry a bomb into the stadium with no one seeing?"

Sarah shook from the stimulant in her system. "D-Damn it, he's right. The bomb I saw was too big to conceal."

Howard rubbed at his chin—now rough with stubble. "Maybe the entire team is involved."

Sarah rolled her eyes. "I can buy one—even two—players being suicidal, but not an entire national football team. Maybe I got it wrong."

"Wrong or right," said Thomas. "It's the only lead we have. Too late for you to get out of the city, so you better pray the bomb squad finds something to disarm."

Sarah sighed. "Then this is either goodbye or see you later."

A pause. When Thomas answered, his voice was thick. "I'll see you all later."

The line went dead.

Mandy parked the car outside Wembley Stadium.

Thirty minutes left.

Chapter 8

Sarah leapt out of the Range Rover and approached the three black-clad men that could only have been the bomb squad. Sure enough, an innocent ice cream van was parked nearby on the curb bordering a large, grassy playing field. A large red sticker across the serving hatch read: CLOSED. Wembley Stadium towered behind it majestically, its iconic arch sweeping through the black backdrop of night. The crowd's catcalls echoed out of the stadium's open roof. The cheers were foreboding—ignorance of the potential danger.

Howard flashed his badge at the bomb squad. "Why haven't we evacuated the stadium?"

"There's ninety thousand people in there." The speaker had greying-black hair down to his collar. Stress of the job perhaps. "Stadium security is quietly removing people in sections, but this is one of the largest stadiums on the planet. If the crowd gets wind of what's going on, we'll have a mass panic on our hands. Ninety thousand frightened people is something none of us want. The Prime Minister demands we take care of this quickly and efficiently. If we can prevent stopping the game, all the better."

Sarah gritted her teeth. "Breslow and her secrets. We have twenty minutes left to get these people out, and she wants us to keep things hush-hush."

"If this is a nuke," said the bomb expert, "then an evacuation at this point will do no good. The evening traffic alone will stop anyone escaping the blast radius. If this bomb is going off, there's no way to mitigate it—thousands of people will die. We are here to stop that from happening. Now, where exactly is the device?"

Sarah and Howard exchanged glances. "We don't know for sure," said Sarah. "But we think it came in with one of the players from the Algerian team."

"Jesus. Then let's get in and start looking. Security has opened an exit around the side. Come on!"

They hurried towards the stadium. Sarah wondered if Howard was as terrified as she was. Her skin tingled, like she was running towards a roaring fire. They headed in through a side entrance and entered the clinical hallways of the arena's bowels. Signed posters of footballing legends lined every wall. Sarah recognised none of them. A team of security had assembled, and each of them held radios. Their bemused expressions suggested they thought Sarah and the others were barking up the wrong tree.

Sarah pointed at the one who looked as though he might be in charge—he wore a black cap that didn't match his blue uniform. "Where are the locker rooms?"

The man shrugged. "Staff or players?"

"Players."

"Right down the corridor behind me, but it'll be halftime in fifteen minutes, so you can't go in there. More than our jobs are worth."

Sarah glanced at her watch. The deadline was in fifteen minutes. The bomb was going to explode at halftime. She shoved the security guard out of her way and moved in the direction he had mentioned. "Let's see if it's more than your life is worth, because we might all be sitting on top of a bomb."

The guard stumbled, and before he had a chance to recover, Howard and the three bomb experts got in his face. Howard gave the man an order: "Start helping."

The guard seemed to weigh up his options then nodded. "Come on, this way."

They picked up their pace and ran down the corridor. Finally, the security team got that no one was kidding. They unlocked the locker-room door and shoved it open.

Sarah leapt inside, hoping to find the bomb in the centre of the room. She looked around. "No, this is the England dressing room. We need the Algerian dressing room."

Howard nudged her. "Do we? I mean, we don't know it's an Algerian player. We're making a huge assumption."

"We don't have time to be politically correct. Racial profiling is all we have right now." She turned to the security leader. "Algerian locker room, now!"

The man didn't argue and took her into the next corridor. He unlocked another door. "In here."

Howard shook his head. "Shit, there must be sixty lockers in this room."

The security leader nodded. "Locked too. Need me to get the keys?"

"Yes, quickly." Sarah looked at her watch. Closer to ten minutes now than fifteen.

"We need to do this now or never," said the greying bomb squad leader, his two men flanking him. "We're going to have to rush any attempted disarmament as it is."

Sarah studied the lockers. The room was large and square, but it wasn't just a locker room. There was an adjacent wet room with showers, too, and a row of large closets full of what looked like bandages and shampoos.

"There's no time," she said. "Get these lockers open any way you can."

Sarah led the way, rushing forward and booting one of the wooden doors. The top half of the lockers were open shelves with hangers over them, but the bottom sections comprised of well-built footlockers. Kicking one was like kicking a tree. "Shit, this is going to take forever."

Working at the locker next to her, Howard pulled out his gun.

"Put that away!" the bomb squad leader shouted. "A gunshot will turn the crowd upstairs into a herd of wildebeest."

Howard spun the gun in his hand and brought it down on the footlocker butt first, smashing it against a padlock. Two more blows and he broke the lock. Once he had, everyone understood and followed his lead, grabbing fire extinguishers or other equipment to use as tools. As the only other person with a gun, Sarah pulled out her Sig and bashed away in the same manner Howard had. Each blow pulled at her stitches, but she was too hyped-up on fear to stop.

But it was taking too long. Four blows to open her footlocker and then met by a large holdall she had to unzip to see inside.

Ten minutes and counting.

Nine-minutes-fifty-five...

The security leader returned with a bundle of keys. He didn't ask for directions and went straight to the first locker and popped the padlock—then the next one—and the next one. His colleagues checked the holdalls. But even with the keys it wasn't fast enough.

Nine-minutes-twenty-six.

They needed to know exactly where to look.

Howard's radio hissed.

"Ignore it," said Sarah. "We don't have time."

"I can't," said Howard. He answered the call and put it on loud speaker. "Talk quickly!"

"Howard, it's Tom. We have a possible suspect for you. Rabah Slimani. He plays in the Russian Premier League. In the off season, he does charity work in Afghanistan—every year since 2011."

"The time Al-Sharir disappeared," said Sarah. "He's our man. I know it."

"Slimani's locker is this one," said the security leader, pointing.

The players had a choice of short or long-sleeve shirts, which meant the ones not chosen remained on the hangers. Sarah glared at the bright-green jersey with Slimani printed on the back in bold yellow letters. "Get it open."

The man did as requested. His hands shook as he popped the lock, wasting a vital few seconds. When he yanked open the locker, Sarah went to look, but the bomb squad leader pushed her back. "This is where I take over, ma'am."

Sarah nodded, trembling with excitement but understanding that a bomb was not a toy. Instead, she looked over the greying man's shoulder. Like the other footlockers, a large holdall lay inside. The bomb expert didn't pull the bag out, but left it where it was and unzipped it. He gave no reaction as he peered at the contents.

"Jesus, you weren't messing around. It's a fucking bomb," said the security leader, but didn't shame himself by running away. He stood rigid as a statue, and so did his men.

The three bomb experts conferred before the leader addressed Howard and Sarah. "This is a Semtex plastic explosive. It's chemically tagged; you can probably smell the signature. Means I'm pretty sure."

Sarah studied the pile of beige bricks—so mundane, so benign. Could they really explode and cause mass damage? "This isn't the bomb I saw. This isn't a nuclear bomb."

"No, it's not. It's plastic explosive. Not enough to bring down the entire stadium, but it's attached to an aerosol and a chamber full of something nasty—possibly mustard gas. We're right under the main stand. If this bomb goes off, it will take out at least twenty thousand in the blast, and probably as many more with the chemical dispersal. The rest of the crowd will panic and trample more victims to death. It's bad. Ninety thousand people bad."

"Can you disarm it?" Howard asked.

The bomb expert shook his head and appeared to grow even greyer. "Not in six minutes. Best I can do is detach the chemical element of the bomb, but the Semtex is wired to blow the moment anyone tries to tamper with it. This bomb is going to blow."

"Jesus Christ," said the security leader. "Oh fuck me sideways. I need to call my mum."

"Calm down, you," said Sarah. She kept her focus on the bomb expert despite the panicking security guard. "What's your name?"

"Mike."

"Okay, Mike. Detach the chemical for me."

He nodded. "Yes, of course, at least we can do that. Then we need to move as far away from here as we can. We have a portable blast chamber to place over the bomb, but there's no time for anything else."

The man got to work and took less than a minute. He removed the glass cylinder full of straw-coloured liquid and held it in his hands like a kitten.

"Who has the keys to the ice cream truck?" asked Sarah

"I do," said one of the bomb experts. "Why?"

"Just hand them over."

The man gave Sarah the keys but frowned. "There isn't enough time to secure the bomb. The timer is set to blow in three minutes. You won't make it"

"Then move out of my way so I don't get exploded all over you," said Sarah. She shoved the bomb squad men aside and yanked the holdall onto her shoulder.

Howard moved to block her. "Sarah, we need to get out of here now."

She stepped around him. "No one is running but me. We can't get the people out of the stadium, so I'm getting the bomb out instead."

"There's no time," said the bomb squad leader, but she ignored him.

Howard shouted after Sarah, but she was gone, racing out into the corridor and praying she remembered her way. She turned the first corner and passed the England dressing room. A couple of physios had arrived—ready for halftime. They dodged out of her way before she collided with them. In the next corridor, she spotted the side entrance they had come through and realised it was closed. Mid-stride, she leapt up and kicked the crossbar-release across its middle.

It blew open. Thank God for fire safety.

The cold night air slapped her face. The sound of the crowd inside the stadium was a force of nature. They clapped as one organism.

The halftime whistle blew.

The deadline was up.

How many seconds did she have left?

No time to glance at her watch.

Sarah raced towards the ice cream van still parked on the curb. She fumbled with the keys in her hand and found a button on the keyring. When she pressed it, she heard the reassuring click of doors unlocking. Heading around back to the large rear door, Sarah opened it and peered inside. She saw a perfectly square box about the size of a fridge. Sarah dropped the holdall inside and pulled down the lid. It clicked into place.

·109·

Please, please, please don't go off yet. Just a little longer.

Sarah needed to pee.

She raced around to the driver's side door and hopped up behind the steering wheel. The engine came to life as soon as she shoved the key into the ignition. The bomb squad kept good care of their vehicles. Shifting into first, Sarah stamped on the gas. The van lurched forwards. She steered away from the stadium-side curb and drove across the road, jumping up onto the opposite pavement and continuing onto the grassy border. The playing field ahead was deserted—not even a single dog walker. Good.

She drove right for its centre.

Shifted into second… third… fourth…

Increasing speed.

The suspension bounced and swayed, throwing her about in the seat.

Sarah glanced at her watch. 9.02PM.

Deadline was overdue.

Sarah shoved open the driver's side door and threw herself out.

She hit the grass and cartwheeled. The mud beneath the field was packed and dry, but the surface was lush enough to take the edge off her fall. She remained painfully conscious as she bounced and rolled, flopping like a rag doll. She yelled out in a mixture of fear and pain, tumbling and tumbling for what seemed like an eternity.

Finally, she came to a stop.

She flipped onto her stomach and looked off toward the speeding ice cream truck. At the edge of the playing field was a row of houses. If the van kept on speeding towards them, it would—

The night sky lit up like a sunny afternoon.

A swirling pyre of flames rose in the centre of the field. All air retreated from the fire, buffeting Sarah like machine gun fire. The sudden vacuum took her breath away, and she lay on her stomach, suffocating, as the world violently combusted. A cloud of dirt peppered her face and made her duck down in the grass. She waited for the flames to take her.

Seconds passed, and she could breathe again. Daring to look up, she saw an almighty bonfire surrounded by smaller, dying infernos. Somewhere distant, she heard people scream.

The stadium crowd.

Terrified, but alive.

I did it.

A lance of pain made Sarah grasp at her stomach. Her fingers came back wet. She took one more glance at the bonfire and passed out.

Chapter 9

Sarah awoke to chaos. Sirens pierced the night and car horns honked like an army of squabbling geese. She lay face-up on a gurney, strapped down around the shoulders and legs. The interior lights of a nearby ambulance illuminated her. She tried to struggle; her body failed her.

"Keep still," said Howard, moving into her vision. He had a sooty smudge on his forehead and his eyes were red. "Your stitches have split wide open and your heart rate is through the roof. That's probably from the epi you stole—yeah, that's right, I just got off the line with Jessica. She's going to kick your arse, Sarah—right after Palu kisses it. He's currently doing a jig around the war room from what I hear."

Sarah closed her eyes and took a moment to herself. She felt no pain, only numbness. Her limbs had been through a spin dryer so badly that her brain had decided to pretend they weren't attached to her. It was a mercy. "Is everything... Did I..." The questions were there in her mind, but she couldn't put the words into sentences. Even that was too much effort.

Howard put his hand on top of hers and smiled. "You did it, Sarah. The bomb detonated in the middle of the playing field. Couple of shattered windows in nearby houses, but no fatalities. The crowd panicked when the bomb went off, but security was able to maintain control. There's a tonne of twisted ankles and bloody noses, but again—no fatalities. Nobody died. You stopped it."

"It's not over, Howard. That wasn't the bomb I saw in the warehouse."

Howard nodded gravely. "I know, but we've bought ourselves some time to figure out our next steps. You have to stop doing this, you know?"

Sarah's throat was dry. "Stop what?"

"Saving the day. I understand why you do it—it's who you are—but your luck won't last forever. I'm with Thomas on this one—I don't want you to die. Don't want you to leave either. I'd be sad if you were gone."

Jessica said the same thing.

Nobody wants me to go.

But how can I stay?

Sarah turned her head towards the bonfire still burning in the centre of the field and watched it flicker. A fire engine rolled across the field with two more right behind it. Had she really just saved ninety thousand people? Al-Sharir was trying to bring the country to its knees.

But I stopped the son-of-a-bitch. However smart he thinks he is, I stopped his plan. He failed.

Until he tries again. He's still out there somewhere.

Sarah squeezed Howard's hand and looked him in the eye. "I'm not leaving until this is over. I want Al-Sharir chained up in the deepest pit we have."

Howard nodded. "Good, but there's nothing we can do tonight. I'm heading back to the Earthworm to debrief. Mike from Bomb Disposal said he'll handle everything here. Good guy, maybe I'll try to recruit him."

Sarah grunted. "No, don't. He doesn't deserve it."

Howard chuckled. "I suppose you're right. The ambulance will take you back now. Want me to ride with you?"

"No, you shouldn't leave Mandy on his own; he'll get bored. I'll see you at home," she said.

Home. Is that what she thought of the Earthworm now?

Howard leaned forward and planted a kiss on her forehead. "Good work today, Sarah."

"You too."

Howard left, and a paramedic slid Sarah's gurney into the back of the ambulance. She closed her eyes and could not open them again.

* * *

The morning shower was sublime. Ten minutes passed without Sarah so much as moving a muscle. She'd gone to bed dirty and wet, but now the soot and blood slid away from her skin and disappeared down the drain, along with the scalding water. Eventually, she had to force herself to step out of the shower and into the bedroom. Senior agents could reside within the Earthworm if they so choose, and Sarah saw little reason to pay rent in one of the most expensive cities in the world when she didn't have to.

She didn't expect to see Thomas standing there when she left the en suite bathroom, and she quickly pulled her towel tighter around her chest. "What the hell are you doing here?"

He looked away. "Shit, sorry. The door was unlocked. I was calling out. I'll leave!"

"No, just tell me what you want. And next time, knock, dickhead."

"I came to tell you we've been asked to send the senior team to Thames House for a meeting with Breslow. I assume you want in?"

"Of course, but I doubt Jessica will sign me back to duty; she only just redid my stitches."

"She's already released you," he said. "You would go anyway, she said, and if the Prime Minister is handing out congratulations, you deserve to be there. She also told me that the strongest pain med you're allowed to take is paracetamol, so if you want to go back on duty, then you have to cope with the pain."

Sarah had woken up on fire, so stiff and in so much pain she thought she was dying. The shower had helped, and now that she was standing, it felt like she might be okay. Her stitches had been reapplied last night, and she slept straight through for eight hours. It hurt to move, but she could move.

"Just let me get ready and I'll be right with you," she said.

Thomas didn't leave. He kept looking away, but turned his glance slightly towards her. "You saved a whole bunch of people last night, Sarah. No one will ever know how close we came to disaster. I just wanted you to know how proud we all are of you."

"We were lucky."

"Lucky to have you," he said. "You're not the same person you were before I left. Sorry I didn't realise that until now. This is obviously where you belong."

"No, it's just where I ended up. This was never where I belonged."

I belonged with you. We were supposed to have a life together. Damn you.

Thomas took a step towards her and turned his gaze a little more. When she didn't berate him, he took another step so he was right in front of her. "If I could go back and make a different choice," he said, "I would. I didn't know what I was getting into, or how much you needed me."

"I did need you, Thomas. But not anymore. What the hell happened to you?"

"It was your father."

Sarah swallowed. "What?"

"Your father was leading a team of SAS and Delta force. He contacted me the day before I was due to travel to Kabul to raid a Taliban safe house. He recruited me en route, sat right beside me on the bus."

"My father!"

"I didn't know it was him, then—not until later when I put it all together. When I first met him, he asked me if I wanted to truly serve my country and make a difference. I said, 'yes of course'. He told me how I could."

Sarah folded her arms, making sure he towel was staying in place.

"A French Muslim UN agent had infiltrated a local Taliban group in the city, and was looking to 'turn' an American captive over the next twelve months. They would stage a friendly fire incident on the troop carrier I was travelling in and then I would be captured by a local militia, who would pass me off to the UN agent's Taliban group. My involvement would eventually get me inside the inner workings of the Taliban and help my country identify key targets. I had to make a decision there and then. Your father is a hard man to turn down."

Sarah nodded, feeling numb. Her father and Thomas had met? Had her father targeted Thomas specifically? Was the plan to hurt Sarah, or was it just a coincidence?

There was no coincidences when it came to her father.

"I can't believe it. He made you disappear. It was him... My whole life, it was him always bringing me down, smashing everything I ever had for myself. Why?"

Thomas shrugged. "He was in contact with me for the first year, but then I started working directly with Delta Force. I never thought I would be gone for more than a year or two, but I just kept getting deeper. Trying to leave could have gotten me killed. Any time I asked to send word to you, I was denied. Thousands of lives were in my hands, my handlers would always say. How could I argue against that? It wasn't until you struck a blow to Hesbani that all of the local cells fell into chaos. I used the chaos to break my cover and return. Sarah, the things I had to go through out there…"

"I don't care," she snapped. "You chose your misery. I never chose mine."

He nodded. "I understand."

"Let's be mature about this," Sarah sighed, "and work together like adults, okay? I don't want to be mad at you anymore. It's too hard."

"The last thing I want is for you to be mad at me. I can't tell you how much you mean to me."

"Thomas… just don't."

"You're still my wife, Sarah. I still love you."

He leaned in closer.

Sarah swallowed. "Thomas."

"Sarah."

He kissed her.

She kissed him back. And it felt like home. It felt like a different life—one with a house and kids.

But I can't have kids anymore.

Thomas pulled her in close and placed his hand against her face as they kissed—against her scars. Sarah shoved him away. "Don't!"

"I'm sorry."

"Don't be sorry. Just be gone."

He did her the favour of not arguing, and with a sad nod, he turned away and headed for the door. "I'll see you up top."

Sarah waited for the door to close and got dressed. Part of her wished Thomas had stayed. Getting her socks on was a bitch, for one thing. By the time she got everything fastened, she was panting and clutching her stab-wound. It reminded her that the Flower Man was still out there somewhere.

Along with a nuclear bomb.

Which is going to strike first?

They might have won a battle last night, but they were losing the war on two fronts.

Sarah headed into the Earthworm's tail section where the bedrooms and staff areas were located. She carried on to the main elevators that would take her up top. A year ago, the surface of the MCU had been a derelict farm, but after the well-publicised victory over Hesbani and Sarah's father, the Earthworm's location had become public knowledge. That was why concrete walls and towering guard posts now surrounded the entrance.

She exited into the paved compound and headed for the barn—one of the few original farm-buildings left in place after the renovations. It was where the MCU kept its fleet of Range Rovers and Jaguars—British symbols of engineering, making the MCU a patriotic force as much as it was a practical one.

The others all waited for her. Thomas looked away coyly, which made Sarah wonder if she might blush herself. What had happened back in the bedroom? He'd kissed her. And she'd liked it.

Do I miss him?

Or do I just miss being wanted? For a second, my scars were gone. I was a woman again.

But then they came right back. I'll never be rid of them. I'll never be what I was.

Mandy opened the front passenger door of one of the Jaguars. "The lady of the hour."

Palu stood next to Thomas, and they both clapped. Howard joined in. Sarah couldn't stop herself from smiling, which left her disappointed with herself. This was no time to celebrate; not while Al-Sharir was still out there. "Let's just get on the road."

"Okay, okay," said Palu. "Good work, agent Stone. I'll see you at Thames House."

Palu got in a car with Thomas, but Howard came and joined Sarah and Mandy. The two cars set off one after the other, with Mandy taking point. Sarah hadn't visited Thames House before, but its grand archway in the city led to the headquarters of MI5. Breslow probably wanted to meet them there so she didn't have to travel to the outskirts of the city and down into MCU headquarters. She wanted them on her territory, not the other way around.

Despite last night's victory, Sarah couldn't envisage Breslow giving them a pat on the back. The Prime Minister gave praise thinly, and the country was not yet out of danger. MCU still had scant Intel regarding Al-Sharir's master plan or his current whereabouts. They were still chasing their tails.

They had one thing though.

"What happened to Slimani?" she asked from the front seat, turning back to Howard.

"Breslow has him. In fact, he's en route to Thames House as well. MI5 will probably take a crack at him before we do."

"Are you kidding? He's our suspect, not theirs."

Howard shrugged, as if he'd already fought this battle and lost. "Breslow works more closely with MI5, and the terrorists wanting her to kill herself has unnerved her. Palu said she sounds ready to start a full-on war with someone."

"Just what we need," said Sarah. "More violence."

"We can help put a stop to it by bringing in Al-Sharir," said Howard. "We'll put that monster on trial."

"Putting him on trial will be the last thing that will happen. It would do more harm than good."

Howard leaned forward. "Oh? Why do you think that?"

"Because a lot of what Al-Sharir says is right," she said. "We have as much to answer for as the terrorists. I still remember being over there, Howard—the looks on the local's faces every time we walked by. We were never wanted there; not by anybody. We can't keep dictating to the world as though we're better. Has Breslow caused fewer deaths than Gaddafi or Saddam? I'm sure the statistics would make for interesting reading."

"You might be right," Howard admitted. "But maybe don't discuss it at the meeting with Breslow, huh? I understand what you're saying, Sarah, but I disagree. We are better. This is a country built on freedom and equality. It doesn't make us wrong for wanting to bring that to places like Afghanistan and Iraq."

Sarah sighed. She hated arguing with Howard—the emotion he put into his responses always made it hard to unleash her true vitriol on a subject. He'd seen as much wretchedness as her, yet he still believed in everything he did. "Perhaps my point is that our methods need to change. What we're doing isn't working."

"I'm with you on that."

"We're here," said Mandy.

Sarah looked out the window and saw the imposing spectre of Thames House. "Are those journalists? They're everywhere."

Howard grimaced. "Guess they want answers. Tower Bridge gets attacked, and then Wembley... the nation is teetering over the abyss. They want us to tell them it's all going to be okay. Either that or they want someone to blame. Keep your eyes forward and ignore them. We don't answer to them, Sarah, okay?"

Sarah's lips were dry, so she licked them. The thought of being caught by a dozen cameras made her scars tingle. *Please don't let me be on the front cover of the newspapers tomorrow morning.*

She stepped out of the car and tried to stride confidently towards the Press. But her legs felt hollow, and she became too aware of her own body. Her approach before the snapping photographers became awkward and stiff.

Palu and Thomas got out of the car behind, and it was to Palu that the journalists congregated with their microphones. "Director Palu, can you confirm the explosion last night came from a bomb intended for Wembley Stadium? Director Palu, is the nation under siege by terrorists? Does the MCU have any suspects in custody? Is the footballer Rabah Slimani implicated in last night's plot? Is he being held?"

Sarah expected Palu to stonewall the journalists like he usually did, but he surprised her by stopping and addressing them. "I cannot yet comment on our ongoing investigation," he said calmly, "but what I will say is that, last night, the MCU's finest agents struck a blow against terrorism. People live today because of the bravery of a few good people. I will share more when I am able. Thank you."

The journalists shouted out more questions and jabbed at Palu with their microphones like a phalanx of spearmen, but he strode confidently forwards. Seeing they would get no more response, the journalists searched for other prey. Sarah. "Hi ma'am, I'm Jack Millis with the Chronicle. Were you one of the agents involved in last night's operation? What is your position with the MCU? Could you share any details with the nation? Are we in danger? Will there be more attacks?

Sarah found herself pinned, journalists surrounding her. She spotted a camera pointed directly at her and panicked. She raised a hand and covered her scars. The flashes came from all directions. Microphones poked at her face. She called out for Thomas to help her, but he continued on, oblivious to her struggle.

"And what about the Flower Man? Is it true you allowed him to escape after apprehending him?"

Sarah's heart beat faster. Her lips moved. "I..."

"Were you involved in the failure to secure this country's worst-ever serial killer? Another victim was found. She died in the early hours of this morning."

"No... I..." She stopped wavering and stood straight. The girl from the sewer had died. Why had nobody told her? Had anyone been with her at the end? A friend? Family? Sarah clenched her fists. "The Flower Man is on the run. I have seen his face, and we will have him in custody soon."

"You've seen him? Who is he? Where is he?"

"He's a sad little man with mommy issues, same as most serial killers," said Sarah, thinking about the girl in the sewer. "He has been living in London's sewers like a rat. But rats are less disgusting. Soon—"

"There'll be no more discussion," said Howard, yanking her away from the bushel of microphones under her chin. "Please move aside. You're hampering a high-security operation."

He grabbed Sarah by the arm and marched her forward, his hand tight around her arm, his voice a whisper. "They're a pack of piranha. Don't give them blood, and they'll starve to death."

They reached the Thames House archway and were met by two armed police officers. No journalist dared approach this close, and Sarah took deep breaths to recover. Flash bulbs still erupted in the road, but now all the photographers would get was the back of her head. And that was her good side.

"That really sucked," she said. "When I heard the girl we found had died... I reacted."

"You did fine," said Thomas, still not realising what had happened. "It's never easy."

Howard rubbed her back. "They don't get it, that's all. They don't understand what we do or what we go through."

"They deserve answers," said Sarah, still hearing the echoes of questions in her head. *Is it true you allowed him to escape? The Flower Man?*

She died in the early hours of this morning.

Palu turned to Sarah. "The British public deserves answers, not these parasites. We will address the nation directly when the time comes. Leave the journalists to make fun of President Conrad. Anything more complex is beyond them."

Palu exchanged details with the two armed police officers and gained admission for them all. Sarah wanted to get away from the piranhas at her heels, so she headed in directly after him, almost treading on his heels. The polished chessboard floor that met her made her eyes blur. The high ceilings made her feel unbalanced. After a moment, she was able to appreciate the grandiosity of the room.

Breslow stormed down a staircase towards them, wagging a finger and pointing off to the side. "In there now!"

They all looked to where she was pointing and saw a closed door. Thomas headed away from the group and opened it. The MCU agents funnelled inside, Breslow barking at their heels. She was not happy.

Sarah clenched her fists. *Maybe she should take on the terrorists herself if she thinks she can do better. Does she think the job is easy?*

Despite her anger, Sarah knew her arguments were false. Breslow did her job and MCU needed to do theirs.

Breslow closed the door behind them and locked everyone inside the small meeting room. There was a television on one side and a moderately-sized conference table on the other.

"Nobody sits down," said Breslow. "This will be brief."

Palu folded his arms. "Prime Minister, I assure you—"

"Not a word, Palu. Not until I've said my piece." She turned to Sarah. "I've been told you were the driving force behind last night's victory. Seems like you pull the MCU's arse out of the fire on a regular basis. Well done."

Sarah leant up against the wall to take the strain off her aching joints. "I seem to recall pulling your arse out of a fire once, Prime Minister."

Breslow glared at Sarah, but then a smile cracked her face. "I suppose I can't deny that, can I? Although it was your bloody father trying to kill me."

The woman had a point, so Sarah shut it.

Breslow stood in front of the door as if ready to batter anybody who tried to make a run for it. There was a reason the woman had stayed in power for almost seven years—she was terrifying. And that terrifying wrath was currently aimed at the people in this room.

"I started the MCU," said Breslow, "as one of my first acts of Parliament, but to tell you the truth, it was former President Conrad who was the driving force behind it. Then the recession hit, and he abandoned the project and left me with the bill. I am not your biggest fan, and this time last year I was trying to mothball you. Public pressure forced me to reconsider, and I admit your role in stopping Hesbani was impressive. You've done good work, and with the extra funding I gave you I hoped to turn a turd into a topaz. Now Tower Bridge is gone, and the public is demanding blood. Then we almost lost Wembley Stadium and ninety thousand fans. I just want to ask you: WHAT. THE. FUCK. IS. GOING. ON?"

There was silence as everyone fidgeted awkwardly. Palu smacked his lips, unsure whether he could speak. "Prime

Minister, this... this is war. I cannot promise you there will never be casualties. That isn't a promise we ever made. Last night, ninety thousand innocent people got to go home to their families because of the bravery of my agents. You blame the MCU, but we are standing in the headquarters of the MI5 who missed it too. We are at war, and the enemy is as strong and as capable as we are. The moment we start lynching each other is the moment they gain a foothold. We kept this country from the precipice last night."

Breslow put her hand on her hips. "Damn it, Palu. Can you imagine what would have happened if the Press got hold of the video demanding I hang myself? The media is running it this afternoon, but I dread to think how it would have gone down if Wembley was a smoking ruin. The rabid dogs would have demanded I actually follow through with it. This nation is terrified. It has been under attack for far too long, and now I hear the maniacs have got hold of a nuclear bomb. Understand this, I will not go down in history as the Prime Minister who let London get nuked. I will not!"

"No," promised Palu. "You won't."

"Promise me," said Breslow, not pleading, but demanding.

Palu hesitated. "I... I promise."

"Then on your head be it. Thomas, do we have any leads?"

Sarah frowned, wondering why the PM would address Tom directly.

"We would like to question the suspect in last night's bombing. We have strong suspicions that Russia is involved in these plots, and would like to get answers to that effect."

Breslow raised an eyebrow. "Moscow?"

"No indication it was government sponsored. It's just as likely a renegade group wanting to weaken the West."

"So, you think Al-Sharir is working with the Russians?"

"That is our theory, yes."

"And do we have a lead on Al-Sharir's whereabouts?"

"Not as of yet."

"Then I think you should bloody well work on getting one. The intelligence community's most-wanted criminal is in our country. If we don't catch him soon, we'll become the laughingstock of the world, or a crater on Europe's backside."

"And we wouldn't want that," said Sarah. "To be laughed at."

Breslow glared at Sarah again. "I see your injuries didn't affect your lip, girl. If not for the fact you remind me so much of myself, I'd wring your bloody neck. Do you have any thoughts about what is happening right now?"

Sarah was unprepared for the question, but the chance to voice her thoughts directly to Breslow was something she didn't want to miss. "I think Al-Sharir has been planning this since the day we took his family. He is fuelled by rage—much like any other terrorist—but the reason he is dangerous is his calm and reasoning. None of this is reactionary. It all leads to a greater purpose. He probably bombed Tower Bridge as a symbol of the damage we have done to his country, ruining it beyond recognition. Wembley was supposed to be a statement about our priorities as a people. He was trying to strike at our obsession with wealth and celebrity—indulgence and sin."

Breslow nodded. "What else is he likely to target?"

Sarah thought for a moment. "You?"

"Me?"

"Yes, Prime Minister. Al-Sharir has attacked our identity, our culture, and I imagine his final intention will be to attack our government. Along with the United States, we have made an industry out of toppling foreign governments with force—Saddam, Gaddafi, our current attempts to depose Assad. I think he will seek to repay the favour."

Breslow sniffed. "This nation is a democracy, not a dictatorship. One cannot overthrow our government simply by killing me. Anyway, he tried to get me to commit suicide last night already."

Sarah shrugged. "I'm not saying I know Al-Sharir's exact plan, but that's my theory. His ultimate purpose will be to punish those he holds most responsible for the strife in his country."

"He should blame the Taliban."

"He blames you."

Breslow sighed. "Yes, I suppose he does. Okay, I suppose we're wasting time. I will give you access to our suspect, but I'm afraid you'll have to keep it clean. Terrorist or not, he is an international footballer. The Algerian government is demanding he is released, and his goddamn talent agent is threatening to sue us all into oblivion. We need concrete evidence he planted that bomb in the stadium, or we'll have no choice but to let him go. A confession would be a very nice start to my day. Do your job, Palu."

Palu nodded.

The Prime Minster unlocked the door and stormed out, leaving them to stand for a moment. Thomas eventually led the exodus, and a member of MI5 was waiting to take them to see Rabah Slimani.

* * *

Sarah stared at the monitor in the open security nook off the main corridor. It showed the feed from the nearby interrogation room camera. Slimani sat back in his chair, one ankle propped up on his knee. Relaxed, confident. Like a millionaire footballer.

"Who's going to take a crack at him?" asked Howard, which Sarah knew was his way of asking Palu for permission to do it himself.

"I will start the questioning," said Thomas, before Palu or anyone else could argue. He strode immediately into the interrogation room. Sarah saw him appear on the camera feed. Calmly, he took a seat on the opposite side of the room's small wooden table. Slimani acted as though he didn't notice.

Several microphones covered the room, so it was easy to hear what was being said from the security nook. Thomas started with the friendly act. "I'm a big fan of soccer. It's really starting to take off back home. In fact, we get a lot of players coming to ply their trade in the MLS. We pay the big money."

Slimani said nothing.

Thomas went on. "There's some big Russian clubs too, though, huh? Like the one you're currently signed to. Was it the money that led you there? I hear you're a good winger; could have played just about anywhere. So, was it the money?"

Slimani sneered. "You may care about money, but I don't."

"Yeah, I like money. Is that wrong, Rabah?"

"Money is a tool to control men and diminish God's influence."

Thomas nodded as if he understood. "It's the only way to buy a Ferrari, though. That's what you drive, right, Rabah? Does God approve of flash cars?"

"Shut up. I don't speak with fools. My lawyer will have me out of here within the hour. I will be out of this stinking country tonight. It sickens me being amongst you."

Thomas leaned back in his chair. "I'm just trying to have a chat with you until your lawyer gets here. No need to be so hostile. Like I said, I'm a big soccer fan, and it's great to meet you. Back to the Ferrari, or the two houses you own... if money is so sinful, you sure seem to spend a bucket load of it."

Slimani said nothing, just looked at the wall.

"My theory is that it's all a front, Rabah. You've been playing the part of the high-rolling soccer player, throwing around cash, jet-setting here, there, and everywhere. You've even been doing charity work in Afghanistan too, right? The model celebrity athlete. Nothing I found, though, mentions you as being a fundamentalist like you're acting now. You haven't preached about the evils of money in the past. Only now, in this room. Why is that? Is it because you've been pretending, but now the need is over? Is this who you really are, Rabah?"

Slimani said nothing.

Thomas nodded calmly. "Did you meet Al-Sharir during your charity work in Afghanistan? Or did you meet him first and start doing the charity work later as a cover? Did he brainwash you into supporting his little crusade, is that it? A shame because you're obviously a talented guy. Why would you throw your life away for a misguided extremist like Al-Sharir?"

"He-" Slimani growled and stopped himself from saying more.

Thomas grinned. "Oh, I almost got you there, didn't I? Were you going to defend Al-Sharir? Is he some sort of hero to you? What were you going to say Rabah? Tell me. Share."

"I've got nothing to say to you. I want my lawyer."

"Al-Sharir doesn't care about you, Rabah," said Thomas. "You're just a tool to him, like money. He's bred you to be his secret weapon—a rich, talented footballer, untouchable by the rest of the world. I have to admit, it's smart. The exact thing Al-Sharir excels at."

Slimani sneered. "You said he was a fool, so which is it?"

"You tell me, Rabah. What do you think of Al-Sharir?"

"Never heard of him."

"I don't believe you."

He shrugged. "So don't."

Thomas sighed. "Look, Rabah. I want to help you. You planted a bomb in Wembley Stadium. Once we talk to your teammates and check CCTV, we'll have enough to bury you. Your government is only making a token complaint, and will give up on you once you look even slightly guilty. No lawyer, or smarmy talent agent, will help you. Only you can help you, Rabah. Al-Sharir used you. Tried to make you a martyr. But you failed your mission, and now his use for you is over. Help us find him."

"I want my lawyer."

Thomas stood up from his chair. "Fine, okay, Rabah. It's disappointing, but I guess your idiocy is why Al-Sharir chose you."

"You'll burn. Allah sees everything."

Thomas laughed. "I imagine he sees far more than you give him credit for."

Sarah met Thomas as he exited the interrogation room. "Is that it? We got nothing."

Thomas put a hand up to shush her. "Easy does it. Breslow said we have to play clean, so that's what I'm doing. He isn't getting a lawyer for at least twenty-four hours, and in that time we'll increase the pressure; make him think we're not observing his rights."

Sarah ground her teeth. "We don't have time for slowly. Al-Sharir's next attack could be in ten minutes for all we know."

"This is what we have to work with, Sarah. We'll do everything we can, but we can't make him talk any faster. There's a hundred analysts back at the Earthworm searching for Al-Sharir. We will find him, I promise you."

Sarah glanced back over her shoulder at Palu. He was speaking on the phone, but didn't seem to be taking charge in the way he should. The man had gone limp, reactive instead of proactive. She looked back at Thomas and glared. "What is going on, Tom? Why are you making me promises and interrogating the suspect without waiting for permission? Why was Breslow asking you personally about the investigation?"

Thomas folded his arms. "Don't worry about it, Sarah. We just need to work together and do our jobs."

Sarah studied Tom's expression, a little of the man she knew coming back to her. He tried to keep a straight face, but the flickering of his lip gave him away. Suddenly, it all made sense. She cursed. "Breslow's putting you in charge, isn't she?"

Thomas sighed. "It's not official until this crisis is resolved, but the Prime Minister feels new leadership is in order. The MCU may have been rejuvenated in the last year, but it still has old blood directing it. Palu isn't the right man for the job anymore—the war is changing. Intelligence is changing."

"You fucking traitor, Tom. Is that why you came back from the dead? To stab Palu in the back?"

"No, Sarah. I came back for you."

"Bullshit. You're thinking of yourself, same as you always did. Palu and the rest of us risked our lives a dozen times over in the last year. You have no right to take over. We're only just getting started."

Thomas shrugged. "It's already done. Breslow will attribute Tower Bridge to Palu's failings and force him to retire. I will take over and renew the public's confidence in the MCU. It makes sense Sarah."

It did make sense, and Sarah hated herself for seeing the rationale. The MCU was bigger than Palu, and it needed a scapegoat to survive. "Tom?"

He frowned. "What?"

"You're a fucking arsehole."

She walked away, ignoring Tom's calls for her to come back.

She went over to Howard and Palu, who still stood by the monitor in the security nook. "We need to go harder at this guy," she said. "We don't have time to pussyfoot around."

Palu looked at her, a pained expression on his face. "Breslow said we have to stay clean. There are no hard and fast methods to make a suspect talk."

Sarah looked at the ageing director and had a sudden urge to hug him. He'd always had her back, even when she'd been a liability. Now he needed her to have his back. "I know Thomas is taking over the MCU and just so we're clear, he can suck my dick."

Howard shot a look at Palu. "What?"

Palu sighed.

Thomas hurried over to shut her up. "Sarah!"

She kept her focus on Palu. "This isn't your fault, boss. None of this is any of our fault. We risk our lives over and over to clean up messes long after the damage has been done. Breslow is to blame for this more than we are, along with the long line of war mongers before her. We are the good guys, Palu, and you are the good-guy-in-chief. Thomas can take over if he wants, but I will never respect him like I respect you, and you are still my leader for now. So give me a goddamn order, Palu, please! Let me get answers out of Slimani before it's too late. He's stalling because he knows that's all he needs to do."

Palu glanced at Thomas. Thomas shook his head and glared. Slowly, Palu turned back to Sarah with tears in his eyes. "I'm sorry, Sarah. I... can't."

Sarah clenched her fists. "Then we're all screwed."

"Hey, pigs!" A voice came from the monitor. It was Rabah Slimani. He was standing and shouting at the camera in the corner of the room. "I want my lawyer now! I'll be free and flying home 1st class by tonight while you head home to whatever slum you live in. Hear me? Get my lawyer or you'll be cleaning toilets for the rest of your careers."

Sarah exploded in a snarl. She shoved Thomas out of her way and barged through the interview room's door. Slimani flinched as it smashed against the wall.

"Hey, dickhead!" Sarah was spitting with anger. "I'm the one who found your bomb last night. The one who made you look like an incompetent idiot. That must really aggravate a competitive guy like you. I'm also a woman, which probably makes things worse."

Slimani said nothing, but the nervousness on his face was easy to read.

"Nothing to say to me?" she asked. "Is that because you're a pampered, over-paid footballer, or because you're a pathetic fundamentalist perverting the words of the Quran just so you have an excuse to act like a colossal dick?"

Slimani snarled, but sat back in his seat. Sarah leaned into his face. "Trust me," she said. "Allah thinks you're a dick as well."

"Fucking whore. Just wait and see!"

"Wait for what? You screwed up, Rabah. I stopped you. Tomorrow's papers will be plastered with your face beneath the headline: Worst Terrorist Ever. Hopefully, you'll be alive to see it."

Slimani laughed. "Threaten me all you want. I'm leaving here, and you won't be able to do a thing about it."

Thomas and Howard appeared in the doorway, but Sarah swivelled and kicked the door shut on them. She dragged one of the room's two chairs up against the handle and wedged it. "I always wondered if this shit works. Now, you have one chance, Rabah, and I'm not playing around."

The man smirked. "Is this the bad cop act? Because I already got the good guy routine off the Yank."

"Answer my question or I will shoot you, Rabah. Where is Al-Sharir?"

"Fuck you, bitch."

Sarah pulled her Sig from its holster and shot him.

The gunshot was deafening inside the cramped interrogation room. Howard and Thomas shouted from outside and rammed their shoulders against the door. The chair wedged under the handle slid on the tiles. The door opened easily.

Sarah pulled a face. "Guess it doesn't work after all."

Howard gawped at Rabah. His jaw dropped.

"Sarah?" said Thomas, standing equally as shocked beside Howard. "What did you do?"

A scream escaped Rabah as he lay on the floor, bleeding. He clutched his bleeding knee like it was on fire. Sarah pointed the gun at his other knee. "There goes your football career, Rabah. Want to say goodbye to walking altogether?"

"Please, no! You're crazy."

"Yep, pretty much. Now tell me where Al-Sharir is."

"Help! Help me!"

Thomas attempted to grab Sarah, but she pointed the gun at his face. "Don't! You've already died once, Tom—this time you won't come back."

Thomas backed off.

Howard remained in the doorway like a statue.

Sarah turned the gun back on Rabah. This time she pointed at his head. "Al-Sharir has taken everything from me, Rabah, you should understand that." She tapped at her scars with the muzzle of her gun. "Behind this pretty face is a monster he created. I am going to kill you unless you tell me exactly what I want to know."

"Help me!"

Sarah shot Rabah in the other knee. "Next one is in your head."

Rabah screeched like a boiling kettle. "Please, no! No, no, no."

"You have two seconds, Rabah. Then I send you to see what Allah really thinks of men like you. Where is Al-Sharir? One… Two…"

"I don't know," he wailed. "Honestly. I don't!"

Sarah tilted her head and pointed her gun between his eyes. "That's too bad."

"Wait! I know his next target!"

Sarah had been a heartbeat away from pulling the trigger, but now she lowered the gun. "Talk more."

Rabah put a bloody hand out in front of his face, flinching as if expecting a bullet at any moment. "He… He's going to wipe out Parliament."

Sarah glanced at Howard and Thomas. She'd been right.

Rabah carried on, his eyes rolling like he was going to lose consciousness. "He… he has a nuclear bomb."

"Tell me something else."

"He's going to blow up Westminster. Tonight."

"How?"

"I-I don't know."

"Oh dear, now you're dead."

"No, no, no. I really don't know. I haven't spoken to Al-Sharir in a year. He… he has been living in Kazan, in Russia. The… the men that own the team I play for… they helped him disappear from Afghanistan. He is acting on their orders. I work for them, not Al-Sharir."

"Russia is behind all of this?"

"No! Just the men who own my club. They… they want to weaken the United States and its Allies so they can take its oil interests and remove Western forces from Russian border territories. Russian crime syndicates want to gain a foothold in Asia, and they have started working together… pooling their resource. Please, I need help. A doctor, please!"

Sarah frowned. "Al-Sharir wouldn't be interested in helping the Russian Mafia. Are you bullshitting me?"

"He's not working with them willingly, but his goals align with theirs. He needed money and influence to complete his goals, so he made an alliance."

Sarah lowered her Sig and tapped it against the side of her leg while she thought. "You're a pretty smart guy, Rabah. Maybe now that your football career is over, you can be a teacher or something."

"I need help."

Sarah sighed. "I suppose we both do now. Thank you for your time, Rabah. Tell my colleagues everything they need to know, okay? Then they will get you help. If you cooperate, you might still have a chance at walking."

"I'll tell them everything. I swear!"

"Good." Sarah turned to the door, but Howard and Thomas were gone. In their place were two armed police officers come to arrest her.

Sarah threw down her gun and got onto her knees. She knew the drill. "Still totally worth it," she said as they descended on her.

As they led Sarah away, she glimpsed Palu standing over by the monitors. Tears glistened on his cheeks, but when he gave her a subtle nod, she understood he was proud of the sacrifice she had just made. Her life might be over, but at least the MCU had a chance.

It had a chance.

Chapter 10

"Be careful with her," Howard shouted at the stiff police officers. "She has a recent stab wound in her abdomen."

Sarah didn't expect them to care about her wellbeing, and she was right. They hurled her into a holding room so hard that she went skidding onto her face. Her stitches were white-hot—burning eels snaking through her flesh. It was hard to breathe through the pain, so she put her hands on the back of her head and stayed there, face down on the floor, hoping they would leave her alone. They were happy to oblige, shoving Howard out of the room and closing the door.

For the second time that week, Sarah found herself locked in a small room alone. Slimani's blood spattered her trousers, damp against her skin. Who knew knees could squirt. She ended up chuckling, but was aware it was only because her sanity lay on the brink. She'd just committed suicide. Might not be dead, but her life was over anyway. They'd throw the book at her for this. The government was all for torture, now and then, but only when hidden, and only against people unable to cause a fuss. Slimani would cause a fuss.

But Sarah felt good. Her high was amazing, like she'd shed a mangy old cloak to reveal a shining suit of armour underneath.

She had stopped being a victim to evil and had attacked it head-on. Her fearful second-guessing ceased, and she inflicted punishment upon one who deserved it. What she had done was not wrong; it was just. Slimani had planned to kill and maim ninety thousand people. Two missing kneecaps was the least he deserved.

Slimani would remember Sarah's face for the rest of his life.

Like I remember Al-Sharir's.

I can't believe he is here. I wish he were standing in this room, just him and me.

For ten minutes, Sarah lay on the floor feeling strong, invincible—no longer a victim.

It had been totally worth it.

Clonking footsteps rang out in the corridor and grew louder as the person approached the door. Sarah climbed up off her belly and stood, ready to receive her guest.

The door swung open and Breslow appeared.

"You stupid, stupid girl," the Prime Minister growled as she stepped inside. She turned to an armed police officer who tried to move with her and waved a hand. "Leave us. Now!"

The officer was visibly unhappy, but not brave enough to argue. He left hastily and closed the door.

"I know what you're going to say," said Sarah, "but I don't care. I'm glad I did what I did. We didn't have time to go easy on that son-of-a-bitch. We needed leads, and we needed them yesterday. Fuck Slimani."

"Fuck you," said Breslow. "Because that's what will happen now. You are fucked. Fuck fuck fucked."

Sarah remained unflinching, even though Breslow's expression made her want to shrivel up. "If Palu and the others stop Al-Sharir, then I can accept a stretch in prison."

Breslow guffawed. "A stretch? Dear, they will throw the book at you. They might even attempt to try you for war crimes. You shot a prisoner in custody on camera. A high-profile prisoner with enough money to create a media circus. They will lock you up and forget about you, just so they can save face."

"So you can save face."

Breslow snorted like a bull. "Girl, don't piss me off. Even if I could keep you out of prison, Slimani's football club value him as a nine-million-pound asset. They will sue the MCU for damages, I promise you. This is a bloody mess of astounding proportions. You've made me look a fool, whatever happens. Saving face is the least of my worries. You think I care about that little shit, Slimani. There is a nuclear bomb in my capital, and it could go off at any moment. That's what matters here, consequences be damned. You got answers, Sarah. Slimani is currently spilling his guts about all he knows, and if his leads help us find and disarm a nuclear bomb, I will make sure the papers know it was down to you. Best you can hope for is that the papers take up a crusade to free you. God knows you're a hero, Sarah."

Sarah frowned. "But..."

"But you're a bloody fool." Breslow reached for the inside pocket of her blazer and plucked out a small black hard drive. "This is the camera and audio footage of Slimani's interrogation room. It contains the whole damn mess. The only copy."

"You're going to destroy it," said Sarah, dumbfounded. The Prime Minister was going to risk everything for her.

"Am I bollocks," said Breslow, betraying her Yorkshire upbringing she hid so well in Parliament. "I will be giving this straight to my Secretary of State for Justice so she can prosecute you for all the world to see. This country does not condone your actions, even if they do get results."

Sarah nodded. "I understand."

"However," said Breslow. "I'm a busy lady and I will be assembling a full Parliament all day today, probably until the early hours. Two-hundred of my peers are demanding to know why our country is under a full-scale attack. I'm not looking forward to giving them answers—because I don't bloody have any. At the very least, I can't see me handing over this hard drive for at least the next twenty-four hours."

Sarah frowned. Is she doing what I think she's doing?

The Prime Minister moved towards the door and banged on it. The anxious-looking police officer opened it in less than a second. "Yes, ma'am?"

"Agent Stone is being released. Please return her weapon and return her to Director Palu."

"Soon to be retired, Director Palu," Sarah corrected.

Breslow shot her daggers. Sarah shut her mouth. One battle at a time.

The police officer looked at the Prime Minister like she had gone insane. "Ma'am?"

"You heard me! Release her now. She has a dentist appointment she simply must get to."

The officer nodded and took Sarah by the arm. Five minutes later, she was outside Thames House breathing the fresh air, a free woman.

For twenty-four hours.

* * *

Palu stood outside, waiting to pick Sarah up. Fortunately, the Press had caught wind that Breslow was in the building, which meant they paid less attention as Sarah and Palu hurried to the car that Mandy had parked nearby. It had darkened and started to drizzle, making the early afternoon more like evening.

Palu opened the rear passenger door for Sarah without saying a word. After she slid in, he went to the front passenger side and got in. Mandy pulled away from the curb. The London traffic was subdued.

A distance away from Thames House, Palu punched the dashboard. "Damn it, Sarah, what were you thinking?"

"I was thinking we were standing around with our sweaty balls in our hands while a terrorist laughed in our faces. I begged you to make the call, Palu, but you didn't have the spine for it. Ever since Tom arrived, you've lost something. Where's the bulldog who helped convince me that the MCU was worth fighting for? Where's the man who would do whatever it takes to protect people?"

"I'm still here, Sarah, but not for much longer. They're getting rid of me, and I don't want this to be my send-off. The world will already remember me as the man who allowed Tower Bridge to be destroyed. I can't let a nuclear bomb slip through my fingers too. This can't be how my life's work ends."

Sarah sighed. "You're over-thinking things."

"I'm over-thinking a nuclear bomb?"

"Yes! We have been kicking terrorist butt, left-right-and-centre, this last year, so why are you now doubting yourself? Because there's a nuclear bomb? We stop bombs all the time. Because of Tower Bridge? If not for us, there would be a dozen landmarks floating in the Thames. We don't win 'em all, but we win the ones we can. Thomas hasn't taken over yet, Palu, so stop acting like he has. You are the director of the MCU."

Palu sighed. "After Tower Bridge, Breslow told me to step down."

"So step down. After we get Al-Sharir. This isn't Thomas's fight; it's ours. You, me, Howard, Mandy, Jessica. We're family."

"And now you're going to jail," he said. "Breslow told me you have twenty-four hours."

Sarah shrugged. "Give or take."

"What you did was stupid."

"But necessary. You want to help me. Let's catch Al-Sharir. Justice will be kinder if I stop a nuclear bomb from decimating London. That's how you protect me."

He nodded. "You're right. Are you okay?"

Sarah frowned at the question. "Huh?"

"You lost it on Slimani. I've never seen you like that. Are you okay?"

Was she okay? She felt okay, but she was still on a high. It was true she'd lost control back in the interrogation room.

"I'm not okay," she admitted. "This last year... Hesbani... my dad. It's been getting harder and harder just to get up in the morning. I've become so frightened that I see danger everywhere. What happened in that room was me finally snapping, but I don't regret it. Slimani is an evil man, and I needed to confront him. I needed to take charge and be the one in control. Shooting an unarmed suspect is not my finest moment, but somehow it gave me back a part of myself. It gave me whatever it was I needed to see this through. Enough is enough, Palu; one way or another I am finding Al-Sharir and looking the monster in the eye. Then I'll blow his goddamn head off. Whatever happens after doesn't matter. My life already ended in a desert five years ago."

"Your life is not over," said Palu. "It's only just starting."

"Then it will be short lived, and I intend to end it on a high note."

Mandy pulled them into a car park. When Sarah looked out the window, she saw a pub named Last Orders. It had several tables outside in a small garden, but with the rain and darkening sky, nobody sat at them.

Sarah frowned at Palu. "We're having a pint?"

"Absolutely. Looks like this is the end of the line for us all, so let's drink to one last hurrah."

Palu and Mandy got out of the car and waited for Sarah to join them. They strolled across the damp car park, the heavens opening above them. Sarah felt her high fading, being replaced by a calm clarity. This was the end of something. Things were going to change. The only question was what things?

They headed inside the pub, where Sarah was surprised to see Thomas, Jessica, and Howard sitting at a round table. Alcoholic beverages sat beside each of their open laptops.

"You were right about the pressure," said Palu. "We need to sit back and think things through in a calmer environment."

"What you 'aving?" Mandy asked them both.

If Sarah was headed to prison, her last drink needed to count for something. "Cognac. Double."

She sat at the round table with the others while Mandy went to the bar. The pub was more or less empty besides them, and it was clear why. The fruit machine was dim and no longer working. The quiz machine displayed an error message on screen. The carpet was balding. The barmaid was miserable. It was Sarah's kind of place.

Thomas glanced at Sarah sadly, but he didn't mention what she had done back at Thames House. He might have even been ashamed of her, she considered, but she hoped it was sadness she was seeing in his eyes. He had gone away for five years once; now it was her turn to disappear on him.

"I imagine your stitches have popped open again," said Jessica disapprovingly.

Sarah nodded. "I'll live."

"You okay?" asked Howard.

"I'm good. Do we have any leads?"

Howard beamed at her. "Oh yes. Slimani would have told us his mother's bra size if he thought we wanted to know it. You completely broke him."

"Shooting a man in the kneecaps will do that," said Jessica. "Crude, Sarah. Very, very crude."

Sarah shrugged, embarrassed.

Howard sipped his pint and updated her. "The owner of Slimani's football club is Omar Vankin, an oil magnate from Kiev, currently residing in Kazan. His oil fields in the Middle-East are hemmed in by Western interests, and his attempts to expand in the region have been hampered by ongoing NATO operations along with other factors. We believe Vankin's connections with Al-Sharir arose eight years ago when he built a refinery in Northern Afghanistan. He entered Britain on a business visa three weeks ago, via private plane."

"Are we bringing him in?" asked Sarah.

"Of course," said Thomas, still failing to look at her for more than a half-second. "I have a team searching for him now. He's not the main thread we're following, however. He arrived in this country with one other person—the pilot."

"Okay," said Sarah. Mandy arrived with her Cognac and sat down beside her.

"The pilot doesn't exist," explained Howard. "At least not on paper. His visa was forged under the name, Karl ibn al-Walid. There's no one with that name living in Russia, or anywhere else that we can find. Check the history books, though, and you might find a Khalid ibn al-Walid. A friend of the prophet Mohammed who fought against an oppressive Byzantine empire. He led a tiny force of Muslims and defeated an army many times its size. Basically, Islam's biggest underdog."

"Al-Sharir enjoys irony," said Sarah, growing excited by the lead. "And he doesn't do anything without hidden meaning. If he had to choose a false name, he wouldn't have been able to resist making a joke at our expense. Maybe he sees it as honouring his faith. He is an underdog seeking to topple a powerful, unjust regime."

"Sounds like you almost believe that," said Thomas.

Sarah shrugged. "I'm past the point of good guys and bad guys. This is personal."

Jessica sipped her sparkling wine. "Isn't everything, sweetheart?"

"Not this personal," said Sarah. "So what else do we have?"

"Omar's plane is parked at Biggin Hill," said Howard. "It's scheduled to take off and depart tonight."

"He might be planning on fleeing," Thomas suggested. "We're not sure."

Sarah shook her head. "Al-Sharir is intending to blow up Westminster. With a nuke, he could hit Parliament from half-a-mile away, but that won't be enough. Parliament must be at the epicentre of the explosion—the exact target—so that his point is made. He'll want to leave it a burning crater beside the river."

"Parliament is in full session," said Palu. "Security will be tighter then it has ever been, in light of recent events. No way is Al-Sharir getting anywhere near it with a bomb."

"By foot perhaps," said Sarah. "But not if he delivers the bomb by air."

"Shit, you're right." Howard tapped at his keyboard. "I'll check flight paths. I doubt any exist right above Parliament, but there may be some near enough to launch a surprise attack."

"I'll ground all flights from Biggin Hill," said Thomas.

"And I'm going there," said Sarah. "If Al-Sharir is planning to commit suicide by plane, then the nuclear bomb might already be on board. We can end this right now."

"I'm coming with you," said Howard

Sarah nodded. "Wouldn't think of going without you."

Thomas grunted, but kept his gaze on his laptop screen.

"Need a lift, luv?" came a masculine voice from over Sarah's shoulder.

She turned to see a familiar face and leapt up to hug the man. "Mattock!" His stubbly chin took a layer of skin from her neck, but it was worth it to see him again.

"Hey, lass. I hear you've been in the wars."

"No more than usual." She eased back and took in Mattock's grinning face. His shaven head sported even more scar lines, and his left cheek had a recent cut. "You, too, by the looks of it. New recruits being too hard on you?"

He grinned. "The green-eared buggers don't know what's hit 'em. I beasted one kid so badly, he shit himself. Other than that, I think he'll make a bloody fine agent. We all shit ourselves to start with if your trainer is doing his job."

Howard stood. "Shall we do the reunions later? We have a capital city to save."

Mattock looked at Mandy who was sitting at the table and about to finish the pint he'd only just started. "Okay if I take chauffeur duty today, guv'na?"

Mandy nodded. "I'll have another drink."

"Cheers! Then it's decided. Let's go and kick some arse."

Sarah grabbed her double Cognac and downed it before slamming the empty glass on the table. Afterwards, she rubbed at her stitches and wondered how much longer they would hold. "I might need you to do the actual kicking though, Mattock."

"No worries, luv. I got two feet."

They headed out of the pub and into the carpark. The rain was hammering down now and forming puddles on the tarmac. A perfect day for the world to end, but Sarah would not let that happen. The sun would rise again on London tomorrow.

"Out the way, please, mate," Mattock told someone walking into their path.

Sarah saw a man in a hooded raincoat and wellington boots. He looked oddly familiar. Gardening overalls peeked out from beneath his dirty jacket.

Sarah stopped. Frowned,

The stranger's jacket opened. "I heard what you said, you bitch. We had something, but you ruined it."

Sarah's eyes went wide. "Get down now!"

The Flower Man pulled a shotgun out of his overalls and pointed it at Sarah. Sarah went for her own gun, but it was too late. She stared down twin muzzles of an antique shotgun. Her death.

Howard barged Sarah aside and dove for the Flower Man's weapon. He grabbed the muzzle of the shotgun as it discharged.

Blam!

A moment of silence, then only the sound of rain on tarmac. Gradually, the rapid Pitter Patter disappeared, replaced by a high-pitch ringing.

The sound of screaming.

Sarah snapped back to reality. Howard lay on top of the Flower Man and knocked the shotgun aside. Blood splattered the ground, merging with the puddled rainwater.

It was Howard who was screaming, even as he fought with the Flower Man.

His right hand was missing.

Mattock lunged forward and booted the Flower Man in the head, knocking him out cold. Jessica, Palu, Thomas, and Mandy raced out of the pub and into the pouring rain. Then they stood there, confused.

"Get going," said Howard, attempting to cuff the unconscious serial killer with only his left hand. Rain soaked his face and dripped off the strands of his brown hair.

Sarah reached for him. "Howard, your hand…"

"There's no time. Go! Get Al-Sharir."

Mattock grabbed Sarah and pulled her away. "Come on, lass."

"Go," shouted Palu from the edge of the car park. "We'll take care of things here. Go!"

Sarah looked at Howard and felt sick. That shotgun had been meant for her. He'd jumped right in front of the blast.

"Go," Howard mouthed the word at her. His wet face was alabaster. His lips quivered, wanting to scream.

He doesn't want to do it in front of me, Sarah realised.

She nodded to her injured friend who had just saved her life, and then turned and ran through the rain, heading for the car that would take her to Al-Sharir.

The boogeyman from her nightmares, finally in the flesh.

* * *

Mattock drove as fast as Mandy did, but with less control. It made the speeding journey through the city a hair-raising experience. Even more so in the pouring rain.

"Now I see why Mandy does the driving," said Sarah in the back seat. She held her stomach, hoping to keep her insides on the inside. She was sweating, and her fingers tingled. After all this was through, she was going to collapse.

Then they'll take me to prison.

She probably wouldn't even get chance to see Howard. His hand…

Sarah's situation began to sink in. She was scared. Shit, she was really scared. As awful as things had been since leaving the desert, it wasn't prison. Would they ever let her out again?

Just focus on what needs to be done, Sarah. Worry later.

Biggin Hill was on the southern border of Greater London, and in normal weekend traffic, the drive would normally have taken two hours. As it was, with the traffic being sparser than usual, the drive was looking to take less than an hour. At the speed Mattock was going, it was little wonder.

"There's a team due in place by the time we get there," Mattock updated her, barely looking at the road. "Got to tell you, it feels good to get down from those hills and back in the field. Teaching ain't for me."

"So why do it?"

"'Cus I'm the only one good enough to make sure the new kids know a trigger from a tripwire. No offence."

"Offence taken, but that's okay."

"So," he asked. "Who was the pillock who tried to kill you?"

"The Flower Man."

"That was him, huh? Looked nothing more than a streak of piss to me. Certainly had it in for you, lass."

"I insulted him to the Press. Serial killers and their egos, I guess. I can't believe what Howard did. His hand..."

"How about you?" asked Mattock. "How are you holding up?"

"People keep asking me that. Do I have something on my face?"

"Just a few scars, lass, but nowt all that noticeable."

Sarah scoffed. "Yeah, right."

"I worry about you, lass. You're my responsibility."

"Why?"

"Because I bloody decided you are. We're not going to let 'em lock you up, don't you worry. I'll storm the gates myself if I have to."

"No," said Sarah. "You stay out of it. It's time I started facing up to things. My mess is my mess, okay?"

Mattock declined to comment.

"I said, okay? You bloody Manc!"

In the rearview mirror, she watched his eyebrows rise in surprise. "Okay, okay, lass. I heard ya. We're ten minutes out, so what's the plan?"

"We rendezvous with the field team and run a scout forward, assess things, and go from there. Nobody starts shooting unless absolutely necessary. Last thing we want is a stray bullet setting off a bomb."

Mattock nodded. "If we get a chance to take Al-Sharir without a gun fight, we should take it. Take that bugger in alive and make him squeal."

The car radio lit up. "Come in, unit 2, come in."

"Sergeant Mattock reading. What's happening? Over."

"Team Leader Fogarty. Shots fired. Shots fired. Permission to engage? Over."

Gunfire rang out in the background.

"Sod it," said Mattock. "Permission granted, but Fogarty, I forbid any of your team to die."

"Roger that. Over."

If it was possible, Mattock seemed to press his foot down harder and speed up more. They had avoided using their sirens, not wanting to alert Al-Sharir upon their approach, but now Mattock hit the button and the Jaguar came to life—lights and sirens emitting from both ends.

In the back seat, Sarah pulled out her Sig and checked it.

It was happening. They had Al-Sharir pinned.

She loaded a round into the chamber.

Time to end this.

Chapter 11

The Jaguar's brakes squealed outside the airport gates and Mattock leapt out, pulling his gun and badge despite no one seeking to stop him. The two unarmed security guards trembling in cover seemed uninterested in trying to stop anyone from entering. Gunfire rang out amidst the din of rain on tin roofs. The rain had calmed, but it had left everything sodden.

Sarah's hand tightened around her SIG, but she kept her finger off the trigger. She wanted Al-Sharir alive, to make him answer for his crimes. Whether she possessed the ability to refrain from lethal force when the time came, however, was unknown.

Would shooting the fucker dead be so bad? At least it wouldn't give Al-Sharir the chance to use the trial as his own personal soapbox.

Possessing the most combat experience, Mattock took point and skulked towards the airport's admin building. His Glock 17 sported an extended magazine and lengthened barrel. The sergeant took his sidearm seriously.

More gunfire sounded from the landing strip around back. Had the field team discovered Al-Sharir about to take off and attempted to pin the man down?

Two women cowered behind a parked re-fuelling car. Sarah slid up to them, keeping her weapon low and smiling to reassure them. Her horrendous scars likely worked against her in that regard. "I'm a Government agent. Can you update me on what's happening?"

The older of the two women nodded, her bagged eyes less shell-shocked than her friend's. Pinned to her navy-blue jumper, her name badge read: Dana. "They just started shooting at each other," she spluttered. "A bunch of men in Hangar 3, and another bunch who turned up in black Range Rovers."

"The men in the Range Rovers are MCU agents," explained Sarah, wiping drizzle from her eyebrows. "The other men are terrorists. You say they're in Hangar 3? Is there a way for us to approach it without them seeing?"

The woman thought for a second and shook her head. "Not really. Your agents are to the rear of the admin building, but Hangar 3 faces it. You can't sneak around because a fence runs right behind it."

"Okay," said Sarah. "Thank you."

Mattock put a hand on her shoulder. "Looks like we'll have to tackle things head on."

Sarah sighed as the gunfire continued rattling off. "It doesn't sound like that's going so well for the field team."

"What are your thoughts?"

"I'm not sure yet. Let's just get to our people."

They entered the empty admin block and soon exited out the other side. It placed them alongside Fogarty and his team, who were taking cover behind an old RAF Spitfire parked on a grassy patch. Biggin Hill had once been an air force base, but this was probably the first time in half-a-century the old fighter plane had seen war.

Sarah slid down behind a stone obelisk holding the brass plate describing the plane's heroic deeds from days past. It was just wide enough to keep her safe, but the bullets pinging against the other side made her feel like a sitting duck.

Mattock ducked behind the Spitfire's tail where Fogarty was popping in and out of cover with his Heckler and Koch rifle. He had three men alongside him, all firing the same weapons, all up and down like springs.

At the opposite side of the paved taxiing area, muzzles flashed from the shadowy confines of Hangar 3. A small plane took up the centre, big enough to seat only a half-dozen passengers and two pilots. Was it big enough to carry a bomb?

Yes.

Sarah's head filled with the sounds and scents of men trying to kill each other. She found herself back in the desert staring at her fallen, dismembered sergeant. It was that moment, when Miller tried to help the veiled woman—Hesbani's sister—move her fruit cart out of the road, that Sarah's nightmares began. The first time people tried to kill her. They hadn't stopped since.

"We count six armed combatants," Fogarty shouted over the din to Mattock. "No casualties on either side yet. We're pinned down and so are they. No one has the advantage, and it's only a matter of time before we start taking casualties."

Mattock peeked out of cover, then ducked down as a bullet pinged off the top of the plane. The old Spitfire was a relic; its days of being shot at should have been over. It highlighted just how long mankind had been at war with itself.

Sarah wondered if one of those muzzle flashes in the Hangar belonged to Al-Sharir. Would this be the day he died? Or the day she died? Somehow, either outcome felt like a relief.

Mattock leapt up on the Spitfire's wing and lay across it, shielded from gunfire by the raised fuselage of the plane. It allowed him to talk with Sarah without breaking cover. "We could call in another team," he shouted, "but I don't like the thought of adding gunfire to a situation with a nuclear bomb. I'll be honest,

I don't know if we can accidentally set it off or not, but I don't want to take the risk. I've told Fogarty and his men to stop firing. Maybe our targets will try to make a break for it if they think we're abandoning our assault."

Or they'll recover enough to set the bomb off right here, thought Sarah. I need to end this now.

"Don't go anywhere," she told Mattock, then broke cover and sprinted back into the admin building. A stray bullet shattered the glass of the door right behind her. A plan formed in her head.

***

Mattock gritted his teeth as gunfire clattered against the Spitfire's hull. A bloody travesty to see the noble machine peppered by a bunch of nationless prats. He'd never understood religious fundamentalists. What were they even fighting for? An idea?

A bunch of children demanding everyone agree with them because their daddy said so.

Idiots.

At least fighting for money or power made sense. It might be ugly, but at least it was understandable. The world was for the taking, and those too weak would lose out. That realisation made Mattock the soldier he was today. Be fiercer and bloodier than the enemy and you walked away with the spoils.

Sarah Stone fought for more complex reasons.

Sarah fought to keep the monsters at bay. She fought to keep moving forward, instead of halting to allow her past to devour her. Sarah fought because she was afraid. And angry.

Mattock smirked. Christ, that girl is angry. I'm not sure she even realises quite how much.

It was Sarah's father, prize arsehole Major Stone, that forced her into a life she didn't deserve. Underneath the rage, it was possible to see Sarah's soft, empathetic soul, but it was covered by so many emotional callouses that it was often obscured. That guarded, yet caring personality led Sarah to join the Army—to 'help'. Misguided, yet noble, it pained Mattock to see what had become of Sarah.

She didn't know it, but Mattock was one of the SAS trainers who had put her through two weeks of hell almost ten years ago. Her father had come to him and told him to make his daughter's life impossible—to 'break her physically and mentally'. Mattock hadn't liked it, but you didn't defy an order from Major Stone.

So he had tortured and beat that young girl—the promising junior officer attempting to join the men-only elite of the SAS. The Special Forces was not something in which you enlisted on a whim to impress your daddy. Major Stone had not been impressed by Sarah's transparent attempts for approval.

But Mattock had been.

Ten days in, Sarah was broken, her lean body an unending bruise after a thirty-mile march through rain-drenched hills. Normally, forced hikes with a full pack were only half as long, but Major Stone wanted Mattock to keep going until Sarah fell. Out of the nine recruits—eight of them men—Sarah was the only one left standing at the end. The ordeal placed her in hospital, at death's door, but she never quit. Mattock had given in first.

As lead trainer, he had no choice but to recommend her for inclusion into the illustrious ranks of the SAS. He'd been happy to do it. Any reservations about serving alongside a woman had been dashed; Sarah was a soldier he would be glad to have at his side under fire. She had done more than enough to earn her place.

But Major Stone thought otherwise.

Sarah did not qualify for the SAS.

But fuck she should have.

Mattock left the regiment a few years later and was glad to see the back of the man who would have his own daughter tortured. He never expected to meet that brave, indomitable girl again, and he never did. The Sarah Stone he encountered last year was a shadow of her former self—impulsive and insecure. Broken in ways Mattock had never been able to inflict on her. Thank fuck he had worn a mask the whole time he'd been her SAS trainer. She never knew who he was.

One day, I should tell her.

I can't keep looking out for her without her knowing the truth.

Where had Sarah rushed off to, anyway? What hair-brained risk was she about to take next? Mattock could not let her get hurt, because he was part of the tragedy that made up her life.

More bullets pinged off the Spitfire. Someone yelled, "Man down!"

Fogarty flew back and landed in the wet grass. Blood bubbled from his neck. Mattock slid down off the wing and scrambled over to him. A few seconds was all he lasted.

"Fuck's sake."

The enemy's gunfire lessened as they started to pick their shots from the shadows of the hangar. Impossible to fight an enemy you couldn't see and couldn't aim at. Mattock had no choice but to call his team into retreat. He ground his teeth. He didn't like backing down—but he liked losing men even less. "Okay, men. It's time—"

Before he had chance to call a retreat, the enemy's gunfire shifted away from the Spitfire and allowed the men to catch a breath. Mattock peeked from cover to see what was happening and was surprised to witness a small vehicle rolling across the tarmac towards the hangar.

Mattock squinted. It was the re-fuelling car they passed when they'd entered the airfield.

The small vehicle was boxy with a bulky compartment on the back. A leaking hose-pipe trailed behind it, leaving a slick trail like a slug. It couldn't have been travelling more than 5mph.

When the men in the hangar realised what they were shooting at, they ceased fire at once. Another second and they might have ignited the fuel container. As it was, the little truck puttered along the tarmac unmolested, driving along by itself.

Did Sarah have something to do with this?

The answer to Mattock's question came a split-second later when a gunshot rang out from the side of the admin building. The bullet struck the tarmac and kicked up sparks.

Flames danced along the line of spilled fuel.

The little truck exploded.

That was when a sleek black Jaguar sped across the runway.

***

Sarah's plan wasn't really a plan. But, she considered fire could only help the situation. Al-Sharir enjoys blowing things up so much, well here you go, arsehole.

There had, of course, been the risk of detonating the bomb in the hangar, but she never intended the explosion to occur close enough for it to be a factor. The fire was just a diversion. A distraction while she dove—drove—headfirst into action.

As soon as she shot the tarmac and ignited the spilled fuel, Sarah sprinted over to the MCU Jaguar. Her electronic ID activated all the vehicles in the fleet which meant the ignition roared to life as soon as she pushed the button on the dashboard. Behind the steering wheel, she put her foot down and grinned at the vehicle's ridiculous acceleration.

0-60 in 4.9 seconds.

The wipers flicked left and right, clearing away the drizzle.

The flames spreading across the tarmac formed a wall, and the little fuel truck popped and spat like a dying firework. The effect was chaos on both sides of the paved taxi area. All gunfire ceased, replaced by confused shouting.

Sarah raced across the tarmac in the Jaguar, engine screaming. With the noise of the explosion still ringing in their ears, the men in the hangar did not hear her coming. Nor did they spot her until it was too late. Sarah slammed on the brakes and locked the vehicle into a skid. Yanking the wheel, she threw the car sideways. The tyres screeched and shed skin as they fought to keep grip. The Jaguar skidded into the hangar at 50mph.

Too fast.

Looking sideways through the driver side window, Sarah saw the plane flying towards her. Two armed men screamed as the car mowed over them like ants. Their bodies helped slow the Jaguar down, but it still slid out of control.

It was going to smash right into the passenger plane.

And the bomb inside.

Sarah closed her eyes and gripped the wheel. Her recklessness had screwed things up again. In her bid to get the bomb, she would set the thing off right here in the hangar.

The squealing grew louder.

Then stopped.

The Jaguar lurched. Sarah's head struck the side window.

Sarah opened her eyes and took a single breath, waiting for fiery oblivion. When none came, she chanced a glance out of her side window. The plane's nose sat inches away from the glass.

Startled men surrounded the Jaguar. White men. Russian men. Men with black-market assault rifles. Only one was different.

One man who did not match his white, heavily-armed colleagues.

Wearing another crisp suit, Al-Sharir cut through the centre of the group of men, parting them to either side. He glared at Sarah through the window and Sarah glared back. Slowly, not wanting to cause alarm, she raised her hands up away from the steering wheel. And placed both middle fingers against the glass.

Al-Sharir aimed a revolver and pulled the trigger.

Kapow!

The bullet left a blackened scorch mark on the bullet-proof window, yet Sarah flinched anyway and threw herself down across the seats.

A moment of silence while she lay face down against the seat. What was happening?

The rest of the men surrounding the Jaguar opened fire, clattering the windows with automatic fire from weapons far stronger than Al-Sharir's revolver. These weapons caused spider webs to spread throughout the car's glass on all sides. Eventually, the windows would break, and Sarah would be a sitting duck. She clutched her SIG and told herself that she would get off at least one shot—and that the bullet would be meant for Al-Sharir.

One man jumped up on the car bonnet and rammed the butt of his rifle against the windscreen. Each blow sent shudders through the glass and widened a small hole right in front of Sarah's face.

Sarah looked out, seeking Al-Sharir and readying herself for that one, important shot.

The windscreen shattered.

Sarah's protection fell away, and the cold air rushed in. The snarling brute standing on the bonnet aimed his rifle at her face and said something in Russian.

Sarah searched for Al-Sharir. Where was he?

Gunfire rang out, echoing off the cavernous insides of the hangar. Sarah rocked back in the driver's seat.

The man on the bonnet flew backwards, disappearing beyond the nose of the car. Sarah stared out the missing windshield and spotted a man in black entering the shadowy hangar.

Mattock.

The MCU field team unleashed hell upon the distracted enemy, taking down three in the first flurry and forcing the rest to drop their weapons in surrender. Mattock moved up beside the Jaguar and rapped a knuckle against the cracked driver's side window.

Vision blurry, Sarah elbowed open the door and got out.

Mattock gathered her with one of his thick arms. "I've heard about drawing enemy fire, lass, but parking yourself in the middle of a gunfight is taking things a tad too far. You okay?"

Sarah patted herself down. Her legs felt hollow. "I think so."

Mattock shook his head and grinned. "You have the luck of the Irish, girl. And big brass balls."

Sarah returned the grin. It was over. They had the plane. They had-

She searched the hangar. "Where is Al-Sharir?"

"Looks like he ain't here," said Mattock. "Sod's slippier than a female fish."

"No," said Sarah. "He was here, I saw him. He was inside the hangar."

Mattock's smile faded, and he returned to business. "Field team, fan out. Al-Sharir is here and attempting to flee."

"Er, Sarge?" A grizzled agent called over from the steps of the plane. The man had opened the side hatch and was peeking inside.

Mattock growled. "What is it, Fletcher?"

"There's no bomb on this plane, Sarge. It's empty."

Mattock and Sarah exchanged glances.

Sarah rushed over to the hatch and looked in. Nothing but two rows of seats, all the way to the back of the tail.

"Damn it!"

An engine roared to life at the back of the hangar. Headlights blinded everybody and forced them to cover their eyes. Sarah saw the blurry silhouette of a vehicle picking up speed.

A white van

The white van.

"The bomb is on that vehicle," shouted Sarah. "Nobody shoot! Nobody shoot!"

Mattock and the men stood down, rifles raised but triggers still. They acted confused, not knowing what to do. The van headed straight for Sarah.

Sarah stood firm, facing the speeding vehicle down. In the driver's seat, Al-Sharir stared back at her.

Finally, they would end this.

Chapter 12

Sarah faced down Al-Sharir and did not move. She did not flinch. The time for running had passed. She would end this now. Al-Sharir must have seen something in her face, because he suddenly seemed unsure of himself. He gripped the steering wheel tightly and aimed the van right at her.

"Sarah," Mattock shouted at her. "Get out of the way."

Sarah stood firm.

The van raced towards her.

After all they'd been through, Al-Sharir intended to drive over her like a stray dog.

Well, fuck him.

Sarah stepped to one side. The van sped through the spot she'd been standing in, missing her by an inch. It carried on out of the hangar.

"Secure the scene, Mattock. I got this." Sarah raced back to the shot-up Jaguar and leapt in. She threw the car into reverse and pulled on the handbrake, throwing the nose around to face the other way. Then she shifted out of reverse and set her sights on the retreating white van.

She sped after Al-Sharir.

This time he was the mouse. And she was the mother-fucking tiger.

Al-Sharir's van teetered to one side and clipped the wire fence as he raced out of the airfield and onto the main road. Biggin Hill lay in the countryside on the south side of London. Traffic was thin here and the roads long, so the chase picked up speed. In a high-powered Jaguar, Sarah had the best of things, but Al-Sharir was desperate and pushed the van to its breaking point. Every time Sarah tried to pull alongside him, he swung into the other lane, or broke hard and almost crashed them both. The few other cars on the wet roads made things even more precarious. Sarah had no way of stopping the van without endangering innocent drivers.

But there was a nuclear bomb in that van. She had to do something.

The Jaguar's missing windscreen allowed the wind and rain to buffet Sarah's face, making it hard for her to focus. What if she crashed?

She punched the dashboard. "Damn it, what do I do?"

It was time for her to admit something. She needed help.

Switching on the dashboard comms, Sarah did the one thing she always felt uncomfortable with. "Agent Stone requesting assistance. I am currently heading north from Biggin Hill airfield in vehicular pursuit of Al-Sharir. I have eyes on a possible bomb and need help. I need backup."

"Sarah! It's Thomas. I have you. What's happening?" His voice was hard to make out through the whistling wind coming in through the missing windscreen.

"Biggin Hill is secure. Mattock is still on site. Al-Sharir got away, but I am in pursuit. Damn it, Thomas, the bomb is still in the van. He has the bomb."

"I have your GPS. Stay on him, and I will send backup to your location."

"As much as you can, Thomas. Send the guy who changes the tampon bins if you have to."

"Roger that. Do you have any idea where Al-Sharir might be heading?"

"Westminster. It's the only place. This is it, his last chance. He'll be heading straight for Parliament. Breslow is there with every MP worth a damn."

"Okay," said Thomas. "I will have all the entries to Westminster secured. Just stay on Al-Sharir's tail."

"You just try to shake me loose," she said. "This ends today."

"Be careful, Sarah. You're finishing this in one piece, you hear me?"

"Too late for that," said Sarah, then ended the call.

Al-Sharir dodged in front of an old Rover pulling a caravan and caused it to swerve. If it was meant to cause a crash, it failed, because Sarah zipped around the slowing vehicle with ease and kept right on Al-Sharir's tail as promised.

You just try to shake me loose, she thought. I'm as much a part of your nightmares as you are mine.

Arsehole.

The chase took them back into the city, and here the dangers multiplied. Whether stressed and erratic, or simply a poor driver, Al-Sharir's van careened and bucked like a branded bull, shunting aside other vehicles and mounting the pavement frequently. Sarah allowed herself to fall back, to drive more safely as she navigated traffic and tight turns, but not once did she allow the white van to escape her sight. At one point, its front-left hub cap knocked loose and went whizzing into the air. Just like his plans, Al-Sharir's van was falling apart. And his frustration was obvious, as with each mile of road his driving became more aggressive—more dangerous. He took turns later and attempted greater and greater risks. He was trying to shake her loose, but he couldn't. He wouldn't.

Yet, despite Sarah's dogged pursuit, she could do nothing to halt the van's progress, or that of the bomb. They were now within miles of Westminster, and another twenty minutes at such speed would see them there. What then?

Would Al-Sharir detonate the bomb as soon as he caught sight of Parliament?

Thomas came back through on the dashboard comms. "Sarah, we have roadblocks set up on all approaches to the City of Westminster. Keep distance and proceed carefully."

Sarah dodged around a post office van attempting a turn in the road. "How far ahead?"

"You should hit it in about five minutes. Palu is leading the team."

"Palu is in the field?"

"I tried to stop him, but this is personal to him too. With Howard injured, he insisted on being on the ground with you. Just keep Al-Sharir heading in the direction he is, Sarah. We will do the rest."

Al-Sharir's van blew a red light, jinking through traffic. Sarah had to kick the brakes to avoid crashing into the swerving cars. "Damn it."

Thomas panicked. "Sarah, you okay?"

She manoeuvred the beat up Jaguar carefully through the two lines of traffic. Al-Sharir pulled ahead, but she still had him. Nice try.

"I'm fine," said Sarah. "I just need to concentrate."

The road ahead was closed. Traffic thinned. Sarah would have expected a jam of beeping traffic, but she saw a man disguised as a construction worker forcing cars to detour left or right. Sarah recognised the man from the Earthworm. An analyst in the field. Everybody was working to end this safely.

Al-Sharir ignored the road closure and sped toward the bridge spanning the Thames.

Westminster lay on the other side.

The road block was set up at the bridge's entrance, leaving three choices—either plough right into it, or swerve either side and end up in the river.

Al-Sharir realised too late he had entered a dead end. With Sarah tightening his tail, he kept going at full speed.

This was going to end badly. Al-Sharir would not surrender.

Sarah spotted Palu at the side of the road. He shouldered a rifle, and other agents lined both sides of the road. Two police riot vans formed the road block ahead, but Al-Sharir never made it that far. An almighty bang and the van's tyres exploded, torn to shreds by stingers stretched across the road. Sarah flinched as the vehicle hitched up on two wheels and bounced up into the air. How fragile was the bomb?

Coming back down on its rims, the van lost speed rapidly. It righted itself just as it was about to tip over, and swerved into the curb. The front axle snapped and dropped the front bumper into the road. The metal strip grated against the asphalt and threw up a cascade of sparks.

The van came to a stop three feet from the roadblock, rain pitter-patting against the roof of the now still vehicle.

Palu and his men sprang into action, rifles pointed at the van.

The driver-side door opened, and a dazed Al-Sharir staggered out into the drizzling rain. He held something in his hand and lofted it above his head towards the darkening sky. "I hold the detonator. Point your weapons somewhere else, or I will reduce this city to ashes."

Palu put a hand up to his men. "Stand down."

Al-Sharir slumped back against the van, panting, but kept his hand in the air. "A wise move. Anybody moves and I press the trigger."

Sarah got out the Jaguar and marched down the road. Al-Sharir saw her coming and smiled. "Ah, Sarah. How fitting you should be here."

Sarah ignored Al-Sharir and headed right for the van. She had to know the bomb she'd seen was real. There could be a timer counting down or a chemical leaking... or there could be a hostage inside. She had to know, and if Al-Sharir was going to detonate the thing here, he would have already done it.

So what was he hiding?

"Sarah, step back, or I will detonate the bomb," he sounded worried, not at all like the man Sarah had feared for so long.

She continued towards the van, grabbing the handle on the side panel.

"Sarah! I order you to step back from there."

"Sarah, what are you doing?" shouted Palu.

"I'm ending this," she said, then threw open the van's side door. She was horrified by what she saw.

Like the plane at Biggin Hill, the van was empty.

* * *

"Where is it?" Sarah spoke in a yell. A yell of anguish, and of anger, that once again she'd allowed herself to be made vulnerable by this man—this monster. Al-Sharir smirked at her, even as Palu and his team surrounded him. Night was approaching, and it felt like when it got there, their chance to end all this would be gone.

"Come no closer," he said, or you will never know where the bomb is.

Palu stopped his team, but approached with his rifle against his shoulder. "It's over Al-Sharir. Just give us the location. No one else needs to die."

"Oh, that is where you are wrong. Some people most certainly need to die." He frowned. "You are Indian, yes?"

Palu nodded. "I am Sikh."

"A people made slave by the British Empire."

"The Sikh are a warrior people, not slaves."

"Warriors without land or rights are still slave. Even now, your homeland struggles to right itself after so long under the foot of this country."

"My homeland is here," said Palu. "And you blame it for sins long past."

"Not so long as to be forgotten."

"The British have never revelled in death. They have caused it, yes, but at least it has not become a way of life. This country is free and welcoming. That is the only reason you have been given a chance to try to ruin it. The men and women of this country are good and decent. They deserve better than to be murdered by a monster like you."

"Monsters are created," said Al-Sharir. "Usually by those with the best intentions."

"Just end this, Al-Sharir," said Sarah, pulling her SIG and aiming it at the man's chest. "Your plans have failed. Be happy that you took a bridge from us. You'll be remembered for it. That's what you care about, right? To stop feeling like that insignificant man I met in the desert."

Al-Sharir raised an eyebrow at her. "Insignificant? I believe I made quite the impression on you."

Sarah touched her face. "What, this? This was Hesbani. He always was the one who got things done. You prefer to talk."

Al-Sharir scowled. The jibe had struck him. "I let my actions do the talking, girl. Did Tower Bridge not teach you that?"

Sarah shrugged. "If that was even you. It could have been your Russian benefactors. How much of a leash have they kept you on? Obviously a long one if they entrusted a nuclear bomb to you. Too bad you fucked it all up. Where is the bomb now? Somewhere at the airfield?"

Al-Sharir laughed and seemed pained by it. "The bomb is where it is supposed to be. Do not count your enemy dead before you see his blood."

"Where is it?" urged Palu. "Just end this now. You will go on trial for what you've done, and the whole world will be watching. Make your statement on the dock where innocent lives aren't at stake."

"I shall take no more innocent lives, I promise you."

Palu nodded and seemed hopeful. "Good. Then tell us where the bomb is and all this can be over with. I'm an old man, but I promise that I will stay the course and see you are given a fair trial. Let's make a true statement today and choose something other than violence. Tell me where the bomb is, Al-Sharir."

"Okay, I shall tell you."

Sarah stepped up and pointed her gun in Al-Sharir's face, blinking against the rain as it leaked into her eyes. "Where?"

He pointed up at the grey sky. "I believe it is here."

Sarah looked up, and her hair blew in her face as a small helicopter whizzed overhead. Nose down, it zipped across the river.

Palu's eyes widened in horror. He lowered his rifle and grabbed his mob-sat. "Command, come in. Aerial threat to the Houses of Parliament. Immediate counter-measures needed…"

Sarah's ears honed in on the whirring of helicopter blades, and she watched as the aircraft cast a weak shadow across the Thames—a sparrow in flight.

Al-Sharir stood at the barrel of Sarah's SIG, a serene smile on his face. "It's been so good seeing you again, Sarah. Truly."

Sarah watched in terror as the helicopter rose up momentarily, before tilting forwards and dropping into a dive. It crashed against the south side of the Houses of Parliament and disintegrated in a shower of fiery debris.

The City of Westminster lit up in a blast. Sarah—along with everybody else—was thrown to the ground.

Chapter 13

Sarah's body was weightless, and her senses merged into a confused blur. She didn't know which way her body was facing when she hit the biting surface of the road. All around her the world screamed in terror, high-pitched and without end.

She ended up face down, forehead pressed against the loose grit of the road. She lay there; no way was she about to get up, wasn't even sure she could. Her shoulder wailed, yanked from its socket. Her stomach sloshed, hot and wet, stitches torn and blood drenching her clothes. Was she dead? She felt dead.

The bomb.

Al-Sharir had played her. The high-speed pursuit from Biggin Hill to Westminster had been a distraction, to keep her and the MCU from realising a helicopter had taken off from the airport. Sarah had chased the wrong goose.

"Sarah? Sarah, are you okay?" Sarah's body felt weightless once more as powerful hands peeled her off the road. Her boots found the ground, and her knees struggled to take her weight.

Palu stared at her, tears wetting his cheeks. "He did it, Sarah. The bastard did it. I let it happen."

She leant into him. "We let it happen."

Across the river, the Houses of Parliament were ablaze, much of the water-side structure transformed into a blackened hole.

The evening sky buzzed with helicopters, but these belonged to police and journalists.

London had been attacked again.

The team Palu had assembled at the road block stumbled around now in confusion; many had even dropped their weapons. Al-Sharir stood in the centre of the road, observing the destruction he had wrought. The sight of him still standing turned Sarah's blood to ice. Ignoring the pain flaring from every inch of her body, she charged forwards. Crunching glass and debris heralded her approach, and Al-Sharir turned in time to see her coming. It did him no good.

Sarah clocked Al-Sharir in the face with everything she had, punching him so hard in the mouth that the bones in her hand shattered. It knocked him off his feet, and he splatted against the van. Sarah kicked him in the ribs and rained more punches at his head. He curled into a ball, trying to protect himself, but she reached down and grabbed him like a child, pulling him back to his feet. "I'll kill you. I'll fucking kill you."

She continued beating him until his face was a mess, and she had lost her breath.

Spitting blood through broken front teeth, Al-Sharir managed to smile. "Thank you for being here with me at the end, Sarah. My work is done"

"I am going to fucking kill you and anyone you care about."

His gaze flicked upwards at the news choppers. "I suspect you shall. By all means, get your petty revenge. You cannot undo what I have done. Those I care about are revenged."

She grabbed Al-Sharir by the throat and squeezed. Harder... Harder...

Palu shouted from behind her. "Sarah, stop!"

Al-Sharir's eyes bulged in his head. The bastard was still smiling.

Sarah squeezed harder still. He began to fade, and it delighted her.

She was playing right into his hands.

Damn you, Al-Sharir.

Sarah let go of his neck and fell away into the rubble. "I won't make you a martyr, you son-of-a-bitch."

Palu took her hand and pulled her back to her feet. He had regathered his rifle, which led Sarah to search for her SIG. She'd been holding it before the blast.

Palu pointed his rifle at Al-Sharir. He was crying freely. "More innocent blood-"

"I already told you," said Al-Sharir. "No innocent blood has been spilled today. The men and women in that building were corrupt. Your Prime Minister has refused to remove her invading armies from foreign lands. She assisted President Conrad in removing dozens of legitimate heads of state, and I have merely returned the favour. Now it is the United Kingdom that will be rudderless, vulnerable to the anarchy it has inflicted upon others. Today, a corrupt government has been toppled, and you are free."

Palu shoved Al-Sharir back against the van. "Enough! Your words are vomit. There is no honour in what you have done." The road-block team recovered their wits and raised their rifles as they saw their boss in an altercation. Palu told them to stand down and kept his glare on Al-Sharir. "You are a murderer. A stain of our world."

"As are you, Director Palu. You serve your own oppressors, and your negligence allowed me to succeed in my life's work."

"Russia will get the credit," spat Sarah. "You're a puppet, Al-Sharir. You've always been a puppet—first to God now to Vankin."

"I am no puppet," he said without anger. "Vankin possessed means I did not. He was my puppet. Look around, what do you see?"

Sarah frowned, and looked back at the Houses of Parliament burning and crumbling into the Thames. Yes! It was so obvious.

She turned back to Al-Sharir and shook her head. "The bomb... it wasn't nuclear."

"It was," said Al-Sharir, "but I removed the core and replaced it. You give me too little credit. Vankin sought to make London a smear on a map, but I kill only as many as I need to meet my goals. The men and women in that odious building deserved death. The rest of this wretched city will be given a chance to change. You may thank me for my mercy."

"Fuck your mercy. Where is the core?" Palu waved his rifle in Al-Sharir's face.

"Don't worry. It shall be surrendered shortly via an anonymous tip off. Weapons of such destruction are not of God, and I have no wish to retain Vankin's property."

"You'll testify that Vankin was behind all this?" asked Palu.

Al-Sharir lifted his chin arrogantly. "Oh, do not worry, Director. I will expose the sins of many men in the days ahead." He turned to Sarah and pointed to the rubble at her feet. Her SIG lay against a brick that had flown all the way across the river. "Perhaps it is best to shoot me."

"I won't make you a martyr," Sarah reaffirmed. "You'll face up to what you've done."

Al-Sharir smiled, said nothing, but then shocked them by pulling a revolver out from beneath his shirt. Palu and the other armed men lifted their rifles in panic.

"No," Sarah shouted. "Stand down. This is what he wants. He wants us to gun him down in sight of all these choppers overhead. His dream is to die at our hands."

The men lowered their weapons, Palu included. They seemed extremely unhappy at allowing a terrorist to wave a gun at them.

"We know each other well, don't we, Sarah?" said Al-Sharir.

"Yes."

"Then perhaps you should have seen this coming." Like a striking snake, Al-Sharir whipped the revolver up and pulled the trigger.

Palu dropped to the ground.

Sarah bent and grabbed her SIG, acting on instinct as she pulled the trigger so fast that she shot from the hip. The bullet struck Al-Sharir's face and dropped him in the middle of the road. But the damage had been done. She dropped to her hands and knees beside Palu and pulled him into her arms. His head was heavy in the crook of her elbow. The hole in his forehead was bright red against his light-brown skin. Al-Sharir had taken away any chance for final words.

Sarah still held her SIG. Now she gripped it more firmly than ever. Springing into the air, a twisted wraith, she marched over to Al-Sharir. The man lay on his back, staring at the blackened sky. He coughed and spluttered as blood escaped his lips. Her bullet had sliced off part of his cheek and ear, but was not fatal. "Ouch," she said, with a hateful grin, "that's going to leave a scar."

Al-Sharir peered up at her. Suddenly, he seemed like an old man, grey stubble and dull, lifeless eyes. The man really was finished. He had not thought of his life beyond this moment. Taking revenge for his family had driven every inch of his soul, and he was now at peace. The Houses of Parliament burned so close that the heat reached across the river. Palu's illustrious career had ended in abject failure, and the MCU's future was all but over. The United Kingdom was forever changed.

Al-Sharir had won.

Sarah too was changed because of this monster at her feet. Her scars were deep, her blood thin. Yet her skin had grown thick as bark. She was a warrior now. Like a Sikh. Like Palu.

Al-Sharir swallowed blood and found words. "Finish it, Sarah.

Point your gun and erase me from your nightmares forever. Gain back your life by giving me my death."

Sarah pointed her SIG over his heart. He placed his arms out to the side, not wishing to defend himself. His sleeve pulled back to reveal a tattoo of a dagger—its tip pointed upwards. Sarah still remembered the first time he had shown it to her back in Afghanistan when she had been a prisoner at his mercy. A prisoner he had eventually released.

Sarah lowered her weapon. "You will stand trial. Good men and women will dedicate their lives to poking holes in everything you stand for. History won't remember you as a martyr; it'll remember you as just another lunatic with a messiah complex."

Al-Sharir sprung up and lunged for Sarah's gun, but she smashed it against the side of his head and knocked him out cold. It fell to her to give orders to Palu's strike team, so she gave them. "Get the prisoner in cuffs and don't take your eyes off him. He has a lot to answer for and would rather die than face up to what he has done."

The agents nodded, but one stared at her, concerned. "Ma'am. You're bleeding."

Sarah looked down at her stomach and saw she was drenched. Blood dripped as far as her thigh. "Now would be an okay time to pass out, right?"

The agent looked at her with concern.

Sarah dropped to the ground.

Chapter 14

Sarah lay on a plastic board beside the road. It was dark, and a man she didn't know pressed both hands against her stomach. When he saw her eyes open, he tried to calm her, and did such a good job that she went back to sleep.

When she next opened her eyes, she was in a hospital ward. It occurred to her that she spent far too much time in hospital beds. She tried to sit up, but failed. Her limbs were heavy, but the feeling was sublime. Although she was awake, the calmness of sleep spiralled around every nerve ending. She barely noticed when Dr Bennet stood over her.

"J-Jessica? Am I...?"

"No, sweetheart, you're not at the Earthworm. You're at the hospital."

"What's the damage?"

"You have a fractured collarbone, fractured fingers, dislocated shoulder, sprained ankle, and severe bruising. You've lost two pints of blood. Oh, and your stab wound is infected. They have you on Morphine and antibiotics. You'll probably live."

"How is Howard?" Sarah didn't know why the thought came to her, but his absence reminded her just how much he had been by her bedside during the last year.

"His right hand is ruined." Jessica sighed. "Lost his index and middle finger. He's being treated at Bart's. You're at the Royal London. He was asking about you."

"It was my fault. He got hurt-"

"Doing his job," said Jessica. "Howard got hurt protecting a fellow agent. He doesn't regret it, so you shouldn't either. You would have done the same for him, and we all know it. You're both alive, Sarah. Be thankful."

"I... am." Sarah's memory offered her something terrible. "Palu! Oh God."

Jessica blinked, and revealed that her eyes were red from crying. "He's gone, Sarah. That bastard, Al-Sharir. You think he would have been content with the deaths he had already caused."

"Did anyone survive?"

Jessica got a hold of herself. "Parliament? A few MPs escaped with injuries, but so far they've pulled almost two-hundred bodies from the wreckage—including Breslow."

"The Prime Minister is dead?"

"Yes. Al-Sharir completed his mission."

"He didn't use a nuclear bomb, though. He could have."

Jessica frowned. "Are you defending him?"

"No. I suppose I'm just thankful the damage isn't worse."

"I've never known you to look on the bright-side. You'll also be glad to know that Al-Sharir has been detained with enough security to ensure he doesn't so much as fart without a witness. He'll stand trial for what he has done."

Sarah took a breath and almost fell asleep. Images of death swirled through her mind, but she didn't allow herself to mourn. Tragedy would fuel her for the mission ahead. Al-Sharir was one general in a war without end. Sarah would see more like him fall. Bradley, Palu, and all of the innocent victims taken by evil men and women would not be forgotten. Palu's career had not ended in defeat, for he had saved more lives than anyone would ever know, and had inspired a team to carry on his work.

His family.

Sarah's family.

When she opened her eyes again, Jessica had gone.

The ward was dark.

Chapter 15

Sarah's first funeral had been her mother's—having died in a sudden car accident when Sarah was six—but she never thought the next would be her husband's. As much as the assembled mourners looked at Thomas's cedar coffin, they all stole sideways glances at her face. The scars covering the entire left side of her face still glistened where they continued to heal. That she was even well enough to attend today was a point of contention with the Army's doctors who had been reluctant to discharge her.

Everything had changed in an instant. She had awoken from a beautiful dream to find her face missing and her husband dead, killed by friendly fire on the same day she had been taken prisoner by a member of the Taliban. The worst blow of all was that she had lost their baby—the only part of Thomas she could have held onto.

She would have been called Katie.

Thomas had often spoken of taking Sarah home to Florida to meet his family, and they had formed a plan to settle down in the sun there, but she never wanted to be here like this, standing beside his coffin next to a weeping old woman who couldn't believe she was outliving her only son.

The minister went on about God's plan for them all, but Sarah wasn't listening. Her eyes were fixed on Thomas's coffin; her sick mind wondering what he looked like inside. The American flag on top of the wood seemed like a cruel taunt, for it was in service to his country that he had died.

Time seemed to slide by in fits and starts. Sometimes a single, agonising minute would seem to go on forever as tears streamed from the healthy side of her face, while other times an hour would whizz by in a dazed blur. This was one of those times, for before she knew it, the funeral was over and Thomas was lowered into the ground, gone forever. Her scars burned constantly, but the pain in her heart obliterated all other sensations.

"I've been so excited to meet you," said Thomas's mother as they headed to the funeral cars. "But I never wanted it to be like this."

"I had the same thought," she said glumly. "Thomas was a good man. You must have been a wonderful mother."

"Ha, never had to be with Tommy. He was such a good boy that he practically raised himself right. Always planning on changing the world. The biggest tragedy of this is all the big ideas he never got to act on. I'm just happy he found love while he was alive. Will you be staying?"

Sarah swallowed. "I don't think so. I... have family to get back to."

A lie. When did she start being so closed off?

Thomas's mother seemed sad, but she nodded. "I'm not quite sure how I'm supposed to go on now. He was my boy. I'm a mother without her son."

"Are you... are you going to be okay?"

"No, not really, but I won't do anything stupid. I'll just go on, I suppose. Until I stop going on. I'm an old woman, that's my only mercy. Thank you for loving my son, Sarah. You made him happier than I ever could have hoped. I know it's hard, but you're young. Live your life. Thomas would want you to be happy."

Sarah reached up to her face. "Live my life? My life was just buried in the ground."

"Yes, I understand that, but Thomas never left you on purpose. He would be here with you if he could, so just remember that. Hold him in your heart and keep being the woman he fell in love with."

"That woman is gone."

"Perhaps for now, but don't let her die, and one day, she will be back. Well, it was nice meeting you Sarah. You ever find yourself stateside again, don't you dare not call on me. It would be lovely to get to know you properly when times are brighter."

Sarah hugged the old woman, feeling awkward. Yet she held on for a long time. Eventually she moved back and smiled. This old lady would have been Katie's grandmother, but now she would remain a stranger. Life had changed course in an instant, and Sarah would have preferred if it had just ended. "I loved your son, Mrs Geller. I will never forget him."

The old lady smiled. "Then one day the two of you will be reunited."

Sarah smiled at the thought. "I can't wait."

***

Three days since the Houses of Parliament had been blown into the Thames and the nation remained in a state of unrelenting shock. In an unprecedented act, the interim government placed the United Kingdom into an official period of mourning—all non-essential businesses closed for a full seven days. The economic impact would be high. But the country's soul needed time to recover.

Sarah stood at the back of the hall as Lord Alfred Pugh took the microphone on stage. No clear chain of command remained, so he had taken it upon himself to manage the crisis by acting as interim Prime Minister. The man had worked tirelessly in the last few days to put the country at ease, and despite his sixty-six years, he barely looked north of fifty with his thick black hair and a bushy moustache.

Lord Pugh cleared his throat and began. "Ladies and gentlemen, thank you for coming. It is my burden, once more, to have to speak to you, but I have some good news. We stand here at our own Ground Zero, where our symbolic structure of democracy stood for over one hundred years. I am here to tell you today that a new House of Parliament will be constructed in its place, and will honour those this country has lost to madness and bloodshed. It will be a beacon of hope to this nation and will stand for the remainder of its history. Long may that be."

The assembled crowd of Press, union leaders, and surviving MPs cheered.

Lord Pugh put up a hand and gained immediate silence. "The perpetrator of this nation's torment is in custody and will stand trial for his crimes, but there are more like him. More sharks in the muddy oceans of freedom. I pledge to you all that we will hunt these men down, evict them from their hives, and put them in shackles. We will put a stop to this senseless terrorism that has come to define our place in history."

More cheers.

"But we will not do so by repeating the mistakes of the past. We will not engage in further incursions on foreign soil. Our priority is to protect our homes—our families. It is not a human right to be a member of the United Kingdom and Great Britain. It is not a right that we will welcome all and solve the world's ills.

The time has come for us to look out for ourselves—to protect ourselves. With that in mind, I am pleased to introduce the new head of the MCU, Thomas Gellar."

At the back of the crowd, Sarah sighed. Al-Sharir would get his wish. The United Kingdom was pulling out of foreign territories and focusing on its own affairs. Sarah couldn't help but feel that was a good thing. Yet, the rhetoric behind Lord Pugh's speech worried her. What did the man actually plan on doing?

Thomas stepped up on stage smiling and waving to the crowd as they applauded him. Sarah also heard a couple of jeers. The MCU was not popular right now.

Thomas straightened his tie and leaned into the microphone. "Thank you. I would just like to start by apologising—apologising to this nation for failing to protect it. The MCU was created to stop men like Al-Sharir before they act, not after their devastation has been wrought. In this, I and my colleagues have failed. But this will be my final apology. I will not apologise for casualties in a war, because such things are not useful. What is of use is Lord Pugh's interim government diverting funds from international peacekeeping operations to domestic peacekeeping. The MCU and associated organisations will be better funded and more highly staffed than ever before. Our failures are behind us, and the next man like Al-Sharir who seeks to shed our blood will be met with unrelenting and irresistable force." He caught sight of Sarah in the crowd and faltered for a moment. "Ahem, excuse me. As the new head of the MCU, I will not make my predecessor's mistakes. We will not react to threats already in motion or chase monsters already in our midst. We will annihilate them in the womb. My pledge to this nation is to make it the safest sovereign land in the world. The citizens of Great Britain will once again sleep easily in their beds. It will take time, but we will win this war."

The room fell silent, not because people didn't believe Thomas's words, but because they absolutely did. This was a new dawn for the fight against terrorism, and the change in leadership was needed. That Thomas had negotiated the MCU's inevitable closure into a rejuvenation was perhaps testament to his suitability for the role as Director. That he had done so on top of Palu's corpse meant that he was Sarah's leader in name only. However, she wished him success all the same because his failure would see the country broken forever. After the horror the United Kingdom had faced in the last twelve months, this was its last attempt at survival.

Thomas concluded his meeting with a brief security manifesto and then exited the stage. Sarah chose that moment to leave as well, limping outside into the afternoon sun which had risen high above the Thames to cast its sparkle on the water. The sun had risen on London again, as she'd hoped, but it was a different city—a frightened city. She was prepared to work hard to dispel that fear, but it would not be easy, and it would not be quick. Now that her own fears had finally evaporated, Sarah could focus on what mattered. Protecting good people against bad.

"Gives quite the speech, doesn't he?"

Sarah turned gingerly, holding her ribs, to see Howard perched on the bonnet of a black Jaguar. Mandy sat in the driver's seat and gave her a wave. Sarah gave Howard a hug. She had not seen him since he took that shotgun blast for her. "I didn't see you inside."

"Mandy and I were listening on the radio. I don't think I could have bared watching it live."

Sarah laughed, which hurt immensely. Her left hand was in a splint and she used it to push against the bruising on her ribs, "Yeah, Thomas was pretty smug. I hate to say it, but I think he might do a good job."

Howard shrugged. "At least the MCU has a future. I hear Pugh might be made full Prime Minister. The nation loves him."

"There's no one else left to do a better job, so I say let him." She nodded to the bandages on his right hand. "Your fingers?"

"Still gone. I'll live though. It was my hand or your life. I'd do it again. Anyway, you look like you took enough of a beating yourself, so don't worry about me. I'm just glad you're healing."

"Thank you."

"I hear the Flower Man is some kind of Climate Change Scientist."

Sarah chuckled. It was a surprising conclusion to the Flower Man's terrible reign. "His name is Michael Black. A meteorologist, apparently. He worked at a weather station in Greenland with a Russian science group until four years ago when he suffered some kind of psychotic break. He went to live with his mother until she died last year of lung cancer. I'm not sure what he has exactly, but it's some kind of delusion brought on by his informed fear of climate change. When his mother died, he blamed the pollution humanity is causing. I don't know, it's a whole thing, but the worst part of it is that he's better now."

Howard frowned. "Better?"

"Yeah, they're treating Michael at a secure hospital. Gave him the pills he needed and brought him right out of the psychosis he was in. Got him to give up the location of three more victims before he went into some kind of daze—won't say a word now."

Howard shook his head in horror. "Can you imagine it? You lose your mind completely, then they bring you back and tell you you've tortured and killed a dozen innocent people. No wonder he's checked out."

"Yeah, I almost feel sorry for him," said Sarah. "Tell you the truth, I haven't had time to think about things. I only returned to work this morning."

"I'm glad you're okay, Sarah. Not being able to have your back at the end... Palu..."

"You were with me, Howard. What you did for me..." She looked at him and sighed. "It gave me what I needed."

"Sarah?" Thomas appeared and joined them. "Thank you for coming. I saw you at the hospital, but you were pretty out of it."

"Morphine," she said. "Because I'm worth it."

Thomas didn't laugh. "I'll be putting a new structure in place at the Earthworm, and of course, I expect you to sit at the very top of things. Not like you haven't earned it."

"Will it take me out of the field?"

"Of course. I'm not having you risk your—"

"Then I don't want it. I'm a field agent. I want to look the bad guys in the face. Give the office jobs to somebody else."

"Sarah."

"Accept that, or I'll leave."

He nodded. "Okay. Hopkins, you have earned a place at the table too, of course. And with your hand..."

Howard sighed. "Sorry, Sarah, but I think an office job is the only way for me to go. You'll need a new partner."

Sarah patted his shoulder. "Don't apologise. There's nobody better to sit in the war room and make decisions. You'll have my back even more than usual."

He nodded. "I will."

Thomas cleared his throat. "I also wanted to talk to you alone about other things, Sarah."

"You mean you want to talk about us?"

He stared into her eyes, acting as if Howard was not there. "Before everything went crazy, we shared a moment, Sarah. The spark is still there. I would like to talk about what that means."

Howard swallowed.

Sarah shrugged. "It means nothing."

"I don't believe that. You still love me. What we had—"

"Is over! I buried you, Thomas. Don't you get that? The only thing I love is the memory."

"I didn't die."

"You may as well have."

"If I could make the choice again—"

"You would make the same decision," said Sarah. "And you should. The sacrifice you made was selfless and brave. You gave up your life, your safety, in order to do what was right. People are alive because of your courage, Thomas, and I don't blame you for any of itl."

Thomas looked at her, staring deep into her eyes. "I never stopped loving you, Sarah."

"But I stopped loving you. You did what you had to, and you made a brave decision. Now it's time to face up to your actions and accept the consequences."

"I thought you'd wait..."

Sarah sighed. "It wasn't just me, Tom. I watched your mother break down at your funeral. You don't get to do that to people and expect things to be okay."

"Sarah, I had no choice."

"We all have a choice. You're my boss now, Thomas, nothing more."

"I'm your husband."

"Until we divorce. I'm in love with somebody else."

Thomas blanched, but looked more aggravated than upset. He had truly expected to get his own way, hadn't he? In his mind, he had foreseen returning a beloved hero.

Howard seemed confused by her statement, and he was visibly shocked when Sarah reached out and grabbed his waist.

He offered no resistance as she kissed him. In fact, he kissed her back for what seemed like a wonderful eternity. He reached up and took her face in his hand, and she let him. When she was with Howard, her scars did not exist. She wasn't a soldier or an agent; she was a woman. He made her just a woman, and that was why she loved him.

Sarah pulled back and stared into Howard's eyes. "Meeting you was the worst thing that ever happened to me."

He laughed. "Thanks!"

"But it was also the best. I lost myself after Afghanistan. You pulled me back from the darkness."

"For God's sake, Sarah," said Thomas. "Will you think about what you're doing?"

She turned on Thomas. "You chose the job, Tom—the toughest job in the country—so I suggest you focus on what's important. I will help you all the way, but we are just colleagues. I want to be able to exist without you constantly reminding me of what I lost, so that I can appreciate what I have. Move on, Thomas. You have a job to do."

Thomas pulled at his tie as if he couldn't breathe. He grew red in the face. Eventually, he turned and left without another word.

Howard touched her arm. "You okay?"

She nodded. "No, but I'm healing."

They kissed again, and Mandy beeped the car horn in a merry tune.

* * *

Thomas turned down the side street where he'd left his car. The black Range Rover sat parked outside a carpet warehouse, out of the view of any CCTV cameras. He slid in behind the steering wheel and nodded to the man waiting for him in the passenger seat. "Thanks for meeting with me."

"Caught your wee speech on the radio," replied the man. "Had the eejits eating out yer 'and."

Thomas smiled weakly. He thought little of his current handler, but was forced to tolerate him and his barely legible speech. "I am in control of the MCU as promised. Am I to proceed as planned?"

"Aye. The bosses are very happy with you. Al-Sharir let the side down by ditching the real bomb, but Vankin isn't ready to give in just yet. Slimani spilled the beans enough to put Vankin away for eternity, so he's had to go into hiding, but the company is still in good shape. Our bosses still want the same thing."

Thomas nodded. He should have been feeling jubilant at his victories, but he couldn't help but be sickened by his loss of Sarah. She had loved him so much once. He had assumed that love would have lasted, and that his return would have been welcomed. Once, the thought of her no longer wanting to be with him would have been absurd. Now, she didn't even like him. It was all Hopkins' fault. He'd gotten to her in Thomas's absence. And now Sarah thought she was in love with the man...?

Absurd. She's my wife.

"We have a problem," Thomas told his handler.

His handler raised his chin curiously, exposing a thick scar across his jugular. "Oh?"

"Agent Howard Hopkins needs removing."

"Is he on to us?"

"He will be. He's smart, and entitled to a high position within the MCU. I hold no authority over the man—at least none he will respect. I want him dealt with before he becomes a problem."

"No bother. I'll inform our bosses. Can they rely on you to keep things tickin' in the meantime?"

Thomas grunted. "Of course. I await their orders."

"The money has been wired to yer account. Makes you quite the rich fella."

"Thank you, Hamish, but this is not about the money."

Hamish chuckled. "Aye, not for me either, but it certainly 'elps. I'll contact you soon." He climbed out of the car and turned, limping on a crippled leg. Before he closed the door, he winked at Thomas. "Bring on the New World, brother, huh?"

Thomas nodded. "Bring on the New World."

Hamish closed the car door and Thomas drove away—off to his new job as head of the MCU. The fate of the nation lay in his hands. And his hands would gladly shape it.

END

ABOUT THE AUTHOR

Iain Rob Wright is one of the UK's most successful horror and suspense writers, with novels including the critically acclaimed, THE FINAL WINTER; the disturbing bestseller, ASBO; and the wicked screamfest, THE HOUSEMATES.

His work is currently being adapted for graphic novels, audio books, and foreign audiences. He is an active member of the Horror Writer Association and a massive animal lover.

Check out Iain's official website or add him on Facebook where he would love to meet you.

www.iainrobwright.com
FEAR ON EVERY PAGE

Printed in Great Britain
by Amazon